# PASTRIES AND PILFERING

## A MARGOT DURAND COZY MYSTERY

DANIELLE COLLINS

FAIRFIELD PUBLISHING

THANK you so much for buying my book. I am excited to share my stories with you and hope that you are just as thrilled to read them.

If you would like to know about all my new releases and have the opportunity to get free books, make sure you sign up for our Cozy Mystery Newsletter.

FairfieldPublishing.com/cozy-newsletter

# CHAPTER 1

Margot Durand stepped off the airplane and into the warm California breeze. It was hard to believe that just five hours before, she had been bundled up and running through freezing rain into the airport after Tamera dropped her off.

She made her way through the airport and down to baggage claim three where her suitcase would soon arrive. As she waited, she pulled out her phone and began to answer her messages.

One text came from Dexter Ross, her newly hired assistant of two months. He'd proved himself more than worthy to take over for her while she was gone for two weeks on vacation, but she was still like a nervous mother leaving a child in the hands of a stranger. Though Dexter wasn't a stranger and *The Parisian Pâtisserie,* her French style bakery located in North Bank, Virginia, was nothing like a child.

He sent a few pictures of the creations he'd made, along with her regular baked goods, and then a selfie with he and Bentley, the shop's daily patron and subsequent leader of the burgeoning senior community in town.

Her phone beeped and she saw it was a text from her sister, Renee, saying she was on her way to pick her up. Margot thought about how good it would be to see her sister and niece, Taylor. Despite the trouble that Taylor had run into in North Bank when she'd come to be an assistant for the summer at the bakery, she was now doing well and back in school studying to be a lawyer, to the shock of her parents *and* her aunt. Margot couldn't wait to hear all about it.

Then came another text from Adam Eastwood, North Bank's resident detective and a special friend of hers. Somehow he had managed to arrange attending a temporary assignment with the Long Beach police department during the same time she would be in town. Trying to hide her smile, she typed in a quick response to his request for dinner that night. She would have this evening free and then the next morning, it was off to enjoy a four-night cruise with one of her longtime friends and the residing French Pastry Chef on a Carousel Cruise.

Seeing her bag, Margot rushed forward and grabbed the handle of the rolling suitcase. Thankfully, she'd been able to pack light, the nice weather on the West Coast affording her the opportunity to wear light, flowing dresses and shorts. She was ready for a bit of relaxing, a bit of fun sharing the kitchen with her friend, and exploring the exotic locals of Mexico.

Stepping out into the traffic of the Southern California airport, the scents of the ocean mingled with exhaust in a distinctly Los Angeles smell. To complete the effect, tall palm trees waved back and forth in the breeze and a man sat on the corner playing a guitar and crooning out a Beach Boys's top hit.

Yes, this was Southern California personified. But after the last few months she'd had, it was time for some relaxation and a change in scenery. Especially after the more recent case against her friend Tamera's new husband George. He'd been suspected of murder and Margot had joined forces with Adam to clear his name.

But that was in the past and now—

"Margot! Over here!"

She spun around at her name and saw her sister hopping out of a sporty, silver BMW, arms waving. Taylor sat in the front seat, her head resting in her hand as if she wished she could disappear.

"Oh, it's so good to see you," Renee said, crushing Margot in her thin, tan arms. "It's been too long.

"We just saw each other a few months ago," she said through a laugh. "But you're right. It *is* good to see you. You too, Taylor," she said, bending down to look in the window.

The young woman grinned. "Good to see you, Aunt Marg. Want the front seat?"

"Nope, you stay there. I'll take the back and get the royal treatment."

Renee deposited Margot's luggage in the trunk and then took off as Margot sunk into the plush leather seats.

"New car?" she observed.

"Dillon," her sister said with an exasperated breath.

"He gave me their old car and got this one. Said he got a promotion or something. How cool is that?" Taylor leaned around the seat to look at Margot.

"Cool indeed." She saw her sister's grin all the way from the back and knew it was a welcome surprise.

"So what's the plan again?" Renee asked as she deftly wove in and out of traffic.

"Well, I was asked to go out to dinner tonight..."

"Oh, oh," Taylor said, "Aunt Marg has a date."

"Is that true?" Renee asked, her eyes flicking to the rearview mirror momentarily.

"It's with Adam and—"

"That cute detective!" Taylor injected.

"And he's in town for a temporary assignment. I don't have to go if you'd planned anything."

"We didn't," Taylor jumped in before Renee could respond.

"Actually," Renee said, giving her daughter a look, "that works out well. Dillon has some work party he has to go to, so you were going to be on your own anyway."

"Perfect," Margot said, feeling excitement bubble up inside of her.

"And then the cruise?" her sister prompted.

"Yes, I'll need to be at the docks by ten tomorrow morning. I'll be gone for four nights and then I'm here for the next week to spend time with you guys."

"Ugh, do you have to?" Taylor said, winking back at Margot.

Renee laughed and Margot felt relief to see the growing relationship between Taylor and her adopted mother. She was sure things weren't perfect, but they were doing so much better than at the beginning of the summer.

Confident that things were going as planned, Margot leaned back against the cool leather and took in the sights of Long Beach as they drove toward her sister's Spanish-inspired bungalow. Yes, this was going to be just what she needed; a relaxing vacation.

ADAM STOOD at the front door of her sister's house

dressed in khaki slacks, a brilliant white button-down shirt, and a sharp, navy blue blazer. He pulled off his sunglasses as she opened the door and she couldn't help the smile that slipped onto her lips, or the feeling of warmth that pooled in her stomach.

"You look like you just walked off the cover of Southern Californian Man magazine," she said with a light laugh.

"Is that a real magazine? Because I may want to forsake my job and move here. This weather is incredible."

"You couldn't be anything other than a detective and you know it," she quipped, grabbing her clutch purse from the hall table and waving goodbye to Taylor, who winked back.

"True," he said, placing his hand on the small of her back as he ushered her down the sidewalk. "But it sure is nice to get a little reprieve from the dreary weather back home. Your carriage, milady."

She gasped when he led her to a cherry red Mustang convertible parked at the curb, top down. "*This* is the rental car the department gave you?" Her eyebrows hiked.

"Well..." He shrugged. "When I explained to the nice woman at the rental office why I was here, she felt obligated to offer me something fun—since I'm here for work and all."

Margot rolled her eyes at his pouty face and slipped onto the leather seat warmed by the sun. "You're amazing."

"Why, thank you," he said, flashing white teeth her way. Was it just her imagination or did he already look tanner? "Hope you don't mind a little wind."

Her hair flew free and loose as he pulled into traffic, but she didn't mind. The warm breeze and feeling of freedom was worth a few tangles in her hair.

"Where are you taking me?" she asked, closing her eyes and resting her head back against the seat to truly enjoy the experience.

"You'll see," he said. She heard the smile in his voice.

A few minutes later, she felt the momentum of the car slow and opened her eyes. They were near the ocean, she could smell the salt on the breeze, but she also saw hundreds of boats in slips, their masts shooting up into the sky. Then Adam pulled the car to a stop in front of the valet station.

With a grin, he handed the keys to the valet and came around to offer her his arm. Margot took in the towering palm trees and the golden glow of the sun making its way into the ocean in the distance. There truly was nothing like a West Coast sunset.

They walked through an open courtyard area where a small band played festive jazz music and then he opened the door to The Bay View, a high-end restaurant from the looks of the exterior. Marveling that Adam was going to such an expense for her, she glanced at him sideways.

"You know I would have been happy with a burger on the beach," she said as they waited for the couple in front of them to be seated.

"But then I wouldn't have gotten to surprise and awe you with my expansive knowledge of—" He looked around the man in front of them. "—cob."

She burst into a girlish giggle, shaking her head. "Cob, huh?"

"Oh yes," he said, standing up straighter. "This restaurant had the best cob."

The waitress stepped in front of them before Margot could refute his claim and they were rushed to a small table on the deck overlooking the ocean. Wine and calamari appetizers ordered, they both took in the view.

"Thank you, Adam," she said, breathing in the warm, fresh air. "This is perfect."

"I thought you deserved a night off before going on that exhausting cruise."

She laughed again, loving the more relaxed side of the usually ultra-focused Detective Eastwood. "I do plan to work on it, you know."

"You do?" he frowned, taking a sip of his water.

"Didn't I tell you? One of my former students, Addie Petit, is the French pastry chef and principle baker on the *Carousel Luxury.* She's enlisted my help because she's receiving an award for her pastry work and they are throwing a large party in her honor. It's a bit of a thank you to me as much as I'll be helping her. I'm not complaining. It got me on for free, so I see a day or so of work for five days on a cruise as a good tradeoff."

He nodded slowly. "You can't just take a break, can you?"

"And when was the last time *you* took a break?"

He hunched his shoulders but was relieved from answering when their appetizer and drinks arrived.

"Well?" she pressed when the waitress was gone.

"I'll admit it, it's been a while. But this assignment here will be like a vacation, I'm sure."

"What are you doing, exactly?"

He averted his gaze. "Nothing too taxing. Just a few lectures and such."

"*You're* lecturing?"

"Yeah," he said, his voice coming out thin.

Was he hiding something?

"On what?"

When he looked up, she thought she saw a hint of apprehension on his features but then his gaze flicker over her shoulder and his eyes widened. "Gabe?"

Turning around, her gaze landed on a tall, handsome man

who struck an impressive profile in a dark jacket, designer jeans, and a button-up shirt with a few buttons left open. He turned at the sound of his name and she immediately saw the shock on his face.

"Adam Eastwood?" he said, coming toward their table, "I can't believe it. What are you doing in my neck of the woods?"

Adam stood and shook the man's hand then gestured to Margot. "I'm on a temporary assignment and…" He looked at Margot and his expression softened. "Having dinner with a friend."

"*Ravi de vous rencontrer*," Gabe said with a suave smile that was meant to convey his confidence with such an introduction.

"*Et vous aussi*," she said in reply, matching his look.

"She speaks French," he said to Adam. "I'm impressed."

"She *is* French," Adam said with a chuckle as he sat back down. "This is Margot Durand. Margot, this is Gabe Williams. One of Long Beach's finest."

"It's nice to meet you," she said.

"I haven't seen you in ages," Adam continued. "How have you been?"

Gabe kept his eyes on Margot an instant longer then turned to look at Adam. "Things are good. Just the same old, same old. Doing the daily grind and all. How are things going with the—"

"Sound's good," Adam said, interrupting the man before he could finish his sentence. "Busy, I'm sure."

Margot noted the awkward nature of the exchange and then saw Gabe's eyes narrow for a moment. "Right, well, what is life if you aren't busy?"

"Exactly." Adam laughed but Margot could tell it was forced. What was he hiding?

The waitress arrived with their entrées and Gabe stepped back. "I'll let you two get on with your dinner, but it was good to see you, Adam, and nice to meet you, Margot."

"We should catch up sometime. Maybe grab some coffee while I'm here?"

Now it was Gabe's turn to look uncomfortable but he forced a smile. "Sure. That'd be great. I've got a few things on my plate this week, but maybe next week if you're still around?"

"Sounds good."

Adam turned back to the table but before Margot could ask about what Gabe had been about to say, Adam interrupted her thoughts.

"This looks great! Let's dig in."

# CHAPTER 2

THEY WERE BACK at her sister's home and Adam had just stepped out to walk her to the door when she stopped him with a hand on his arm. The bright moonlight warred for attention with the streetlights running down the street and, if it were possible, Margot thought the weather had gotten even warmer while they had dinner.

"Adam," she said, sliding her hand from his forearm down to this hand, "are you going to tell me what you kept Gabe from saying at dinner tonight?"

He feigned a look of confusion. "Gabe? What do you mean? Was he saying something?"

"Are you going to stand there and lie to my face, Adam Eastwood? Because if so, I'm going inside and you may never hear from me again." Though her words held weight, she kept them light. He was silent for so long she grew more frustrated and started to turn.

"Margot," he said, pulling her back and gripping her hand more firmly, "just hold on."

"I don't like secrets," she said. "And, maybe I'm foolish for thinking this, but I thought things between us were going...well. Maybe I'm just kidding myself and you can stop me right here if I'm wrong, but—"

"You're not wrong." His words effectively silenced her. "But..." He looked up, his gaze trailing down the street then back to her. "There are things that I won't—*can't*—share with you. At least not yet."

She understood the silence of his career. A detective held many things close to the vest, something she'd experienced firsthand with her late husband Julian, but this felt worse somehow. They weren't in North Bank, what could he be hiding from her here?

"Your buddy can know these things but I can't?"

He grimaced. "Look, I want you to trust me. Not just as a detective in your hometown, but as a friend and...maybe as more someday." He took a breath. "And believe me, when I can tell you, I will, but I can't. Not yet. I'm sorry."

"So you're not going to tell me?"

"Not yet." He grimaced but she could tell, despite his tightlipped response, that he *wanted* to tell her. At least it seemed that way.

"I understand."

He opened his mouth as if prepared for an argument but then closed it. "You do?"

"I do."

"Margot, have I told you how amazing you are?"

She laughed and shook her head. "You've resorted to flattery, Detective Eastwood? I thought that was below you."

"Never," he said, pulling her closer.

Her breath caught at his sudden nearness and she was aware of how warm and comforting his hand felt wrapped around hers. She craved that comfort more than she wanted to admit.

When they had finished the last case exonerating her best friend's husband from a murder charge, Adam had taken her out for their first official date. That had been just over two months ago, but she still wasn't sure what *they* were. A couple? Just dating? Even more? He'd called her his friend to Gabe Williams...

Her mind drew back to the present and the reality that Adam was drawing closer to her. Her heartbeat thundered in her chest but she didn't draw away. She didn't want to. They had only kissed one other time in a stolen moment after a street festival in DC. The festival had been interrupted by rain and they'd taken cover under an awning, drawing close to stay out of the downpour.

But now, after a romantic dinner and in the warm breeze

swirling around them, she wanted to experience that again. To feel his lips, soft but strong on hers. And the next instant, she did.

Her eyelids fluttered closed and his free hand wrapped around her, pressing gently against the small of her back. His fingers were warm through the silky fabric of her summer dress and the spicy scent of his cologne intermingled with the flowery scent of her perfume.

The kiss was short but not without its own type of passion. Tender, but firm; sweet, but short. His lips gone from hers much too quickly.

"Have a good cruise, Margot," he said. His breath fanned out warm against her cheeks.

"Have fun teaching, Professor Eastwood." His deep chuckle broke some of the spell and she stepped back to head toward the house. "I will. And, Margot—"

She looked up at him.

"I'll tell you when I can."

"You'd better."

THE NEXT MORNING dawned bright but subtly cooler than the previous day. Margot didn't mind, but knowing that it would be even cooler on the ship, she pulled a lightweight, striped sweatshirt over jean capris with comfortable, cushioned flats to finish off the ensemble.

Then, making sure she'd repacked everything she'd need on the cruise, she followed Renee out the door.

"Have fun and *relax*," her sister said when she dropped her off at the docks.

"Tell Taylor and Dillon bye for me. I'll see you all when I get back."

Margot pulled her large canvas purse higher on her shoulder and toted her rolling suitcase behind her as she made her way toward the large ship sparkling in the morning sunlight.

The *Carousel Luxury,* the finest in its fleet, rose up in front of her to a stunning height of fifteen floors for the cabin area with a length of over one thousand feet. The bright yellow and red flags stuck out against the gleaming white sides of the massive ship and flapped wildly in the wind. She felt like an ant the closer she came.

"Hello, ma'am," a kind looking older man said. He wore longer, white shorts and a white, button-up shirt with a badge that read "Jack" and held a clipboard in his hand. "How can I direct you?"

She showed him her ticket, uncertain of where she was supposed to go.

"Oh, you're here to help Miss Petit? Wonderful," he said, his smile widening, if that were possible. "Let me get someone to show you to the right entrance. Just one moment."

She nodded and watched as he keyed into a microphone attached to a radio. Soon a younger man came and led her to a gangplank that appeared to be the crew's entrance. "Right this way, ma'am," the young man said.

She followed him up the ramp and soon they were stepping into a room where a woman sat behind a desk looking slightly harried.

"Phillip, I thought I told you not to—" When she looked up, she stopped and pressed her lips into a smile. "I'm sorry, I didn't know you had brought a guest on board." Her gaze flickered to the young man at Margot's side and he rushed to explain.

"This is Miss Petit's guest for the week."

The woman flashed a forced smile at Margot and turned several pages in a thick binder in front of her. "Ah, Mrs. Durand?"

"Yes," Margot said.

"Welcome aboard." She looked to the young man, "You're dismissed, Phillip. I'll take Mrs. Durand to her room." Standing, she turned back to Margot. "I'm Sophia and I'll take you to your room if you'll follow me?"

Margot did, rolling her suitcase behind her as they turned down a long corridor.

"Your cabin has a lovely view of the water. I'm sure you'll be very happy with it."

"Thank you very much," Margot said, picking up her pace to match that of the woman.

They turned down one more hall before the woman pulled up short. "Ah, here we are." Retrieving a keycard, she opened the door and pushed it in. "Welcome to your suite, Mrs. Durand."

Margot gasped as she stepped past the woman into the ocean view room. She hadn't expected this. When she'd agreed to Addie's pleading to join her on a cruise, she'd thought the room would be in the interior and just big enough to fit a bed, but this room exceeded any idea she'd had.

It wasn't large by any standard, but it was bright and cheery, with an incredible view just as the stewardess had said. The sliding glass door led out onto a tiny deck with two chairs. Inside, a queen-sized bed took over the space of one wall with a small couch and chair at its foot. The tiny bathroom sat to the left with a closet next to it and then a desk next to that. Everything she needed —and more.

"This is lovely. Thank you."

The woman gave a brisk nod and handed her some papers. "Here is a map of the ship. I've indicated here, here, and here—" She pointed to the paper. "—where the kitchen and bake shop are located. You'll likely find her in the kitchen at this hour. This special keycard will get you there."

Sophia looked up and flashed another business-like smile before motioning to close the door.

"Uh, Sophia?"

The woman stopped, her mask of helpfulness firmly in place.

"Thank you, for all of this. I really appreciate the hard work you've done. I hope today isn't too stressful for you."

The woman seemed taken off guard but a real smile broke through. "One of our senior crew members is out sick for this cruise so things are a little…crazy," she said, breaking her business-like manner. "Thank you. I really hope you have a great time."

Margot watched her go then closed the door and sunk down onto the plush bed.

"Oh, I think I will," she said to the stillness of the room before she fell back against the cushions.

"I'M NOT sure what to do, Noah. I am one hundred and twenty percent certain I ordered more than enough, but I'm not seeing it on this inventory sheet. And where in the world are my other boxes?"

Margot smiled as she came around the corner into the commercial grade kitchen. She'd recognize that voice anywhere.

"Miss Petit," she said in her sternest teacher's voice.

The young woman, now in her early thirties, turned around, her dark brown hair pulled back into a tight French twist.

"Margot!" she screamed and rushed at her with open arms. "You're here!"

Margot laughed, hugging the woman back with equal force. "As if I'd miss this trip."

"I'm so glad you could come. Are you *sure* you don't mind helping me?"

"I am more than happy to do whatever you need me to. I'm at your beck and call."

The woman laughed, the sound like tiny silver bells, as she clasped Margot's hands.

"No, no! None of that. You are here to help me with the gala and awards ceremony, but in every other respect, you are our guest." The young man behind Addie coughed. "Oh goodness! I'm so sorry. Margot Durand, this is Noah Spence, he's my right-hand man."

"Pleased to meet you, Mrs. Durand. Addie has told me a lot about you."

The handsome young man smiled back at her, showing off deep dimples. He was handsome in a boyish way and when he turned his gaze on Addie, she wondered if they were more than friends. She filed the information away to ask her friend about later.

"It's nice to meet you too, Noah. Have you worked on board this ship long?"

"About three years now," he said, grinning at Addie. "Though this boss of mine has made it feel like more."

"Oh, don't listen to him," Addie said, laughing. "He's a great pastry chef in his own right and I'm lucky to have him on my team. So, are you ready to get the grand tour?"

Margot looked between Addie and Noah. "Can you get away like this?"

Addie laughed. "I'm a pastry chef, not a prisoner. And yes, we've been prepping early—baker's hours," she said with a wink at Margot, "and the guests won't all be on board for several more hours. It'll be relatively quiet. The perfect time for a tour."

"Great," Margot said, "lead the way, Chef."

Addie paused, closing her eyes and holding her hands out.

"What are you doing?" Noah asked, looking skeptical.

"Just basking in the moment that my most formidable, and most talented, teacher called me Chef. I have arrived."

The three of them laughed and Noah gave her a gentle shove. "Go on then."

They walked back out into the hallway and she turned to look at Margot. "What have you seen so far?"

"Seen?" Margot said, looking doubtful. "The hallway and my room."

"Got it," Addie said, grinning. "Then we'll head to the mezzanine and you can see what most people see first."

As they walked, Margot asked Addie to fill her in on the years since she had graduated from the institute that Margot had taught at. Filled with internships and jobs in well-known French bakeries in Paris, Addie then made her way to the West Coast where she gained employment with *Carousel* on their primary luxury ship.

"Will you be going back to France?" Margot asked when Addie had finished her litany of jobs.

She smiled. "I'm not sure. I'll have to wait and see how things turn out here."

There was something in the girl's smile that reminded Margot of how she'd acted when she'd been in love with Julian. "Addie, is there something you're not telling me?"

The girl's face blanched. "Not…telling you?"

"Is there—"

"Oh, *there* you are," said a loud, booming voice.

Both women jumped and turned to see a man dressed in dark pants, a white shirt, and a navy blue vest. He carried a folder with him and looked to be in a hurry.

"Please tell me you've made all of the arrangements for the gala. We set sail in less than five hours."

"Michael," Addie said, resting her hand over her heart, "I sent you a text not an hour ago telling you what I still needed. Somehow I've got supplies missing, though I don't know how that's possible. You replied that you were on it. Is that not true?"

The man stuttered. "I-I did?"

"Yes." Addie sighed then turned to look at Margot. "Would you give us a minute? The mezzanine is just that way. Feel free to look around, though I don't think any of the shops will be open yet."

"Take your time," Margot said and then slipped past them.

As she walked away, she heard them lower their voices as they compared notes. It was interesting that, on such a large ship with such limited access, Addie would find things missing from her kitchen. Or was it called a galley?

Margot smiled to herself but it soon turned into a gasp. As she pushed through two double glass doors, she was stunned with the beauty of the mezzanine. Against the far wall was a glass-fronted elevator that looked like it ran to the top floors of the ship. Then, in a circular space surrounding the open lobby-like area, Margot saw couches and reading nooks, small tables, and shop fronts surrounding the lower floor.

As she looked higher, she saw that at least three of the

lower floors were open, accessed by elevators or a staircase that sat at the far side. The décor was a gaudy mix of deep reds and golden yellows with accents of navy blue. Vibrant green plants dotted the sitting areas and the dim but plentiful lights sparkled off the gold surfaces. It really was a sight to behold.

"Sorry about that," Addie said, coming up behind Margot.

"That didn't take long."

She rolled her eyes. "He's taking over for one of our senior crew members—"

"The one who's out sick?"

Addie looked surprised. "How did you know?"

Not wanting to get the woman in trouble, in case that type of information was classified, she just smiled. "I heard a rumor."

"It's so sad, Alison is great—super organized and always on top of things—but she came down with something awful last night. When I got the text, I knew it was going to be crazy today. I just didn't expect this. Michael's been trying to slip into her spot for a while now—always showing up where he doesn't belong—and now this. I'm afraid the power will go to his head."

"How did you know she was going to be gone? She texted you?"

"We're friends," Addie said, smiling. "We do yoga together

in the mornings—there's a great class on board. You should totally join."

Margot merely smiled at this.

"But yeah, she was feeling fine then suddenly she's sick. It's bizarre. I mean, Michael's a good guy but he's… overzealous to put it mildly. And he's also nowhere near as organized as Ali."

"Do you have what you need? I heard you say something about missing supplies."

Addie shrugged. "He says he'll get it here. The thing I don't get is *how* I'm missing flour. It's not like anyone is going to use extra bags of flour. Maybe I just miscalculated. Anyway, let's continue the tour and then grab lunch. We have the *best* food on board the *Carousel Luxury.*"

Margot had heard as much and agreed. "I'm ready to get to the relaxing part of this cruise. Lead the way."

# CHAPTER 3

A NEW DAY dawned and found the *Carousel Luxury* cutting deftly through the vibrant, aqua blue ocean on its way toward Mexico and the port of Ensenada. Margot hadn't been to Mexico before and she was thrilled with the thought of exploring the touristy city. If she'd been traveling on her own and not with a cruise line, she might have considered a foray into the wilds of the land, seeing the true side of Mexico that she'd read about, but as it was, she and all passengers like her would be relegated to specific areas.

She pushed the thoughts of exploration aside as she strode out onto the wood deck and searched the area for a free chaise lounge. They wouldn't be in Mexico until the next day so she had no reason to think about what she would do until the next day. Wasn't that the luxury of the cruise? To relax, eat, and push worries to the side?

She'd donned shorts and a tank top, forgoing her

swimsuit seeing as how a slight haze still clung to the morning sky. It was warm enough in the sun, but she wouldn't be swimming. Instead, she'd packed a few novels. All thrillers, all involving crime, and all guaranteed to grip her attention no matter how distracting the activities of the deck became.

Fortunately, since it was still early, there were fewer people out and she was able to snag a chair overlooking the vast ocean as it slipped past. Reclining back and donning a floppy straw hat, she smiled to herself. *This* was perfection. The salty breeze played with the towel she'd tossed over her legs to ward off the nip in the air, but her attention was arrested by the horizon that met the sky in a gentle kiss. A perfect mingling of blues.

Reaching into her bag, she pulled out the newest Baldacci thriller and opened to the first chapter. She relished the feel of the trade paperback in her fingers; the thick weight of the book in her hand promising adventures one right after the other. She'd just started into the first paragraph when a shadow fell over her towel-draped legs.

"I'm fine, thank you," she said without looking up. She knew the stewards were good at their jobs. They were present and helpful, but at this moment they were being *too* helpful. She didn't want or need anything aside from silence and peace.

The shadow didn't move.

Closing her eyes and taking in a deep breath, Margot

fought the urge to continue to ignore the shadow. They would go away eventually, wouldn't they?

"I think you've mistaken me for someone else," a deep voice said.

Now she rolled her eyes. The action was hidden by her hat from the man whose voice she'd heard, but she was tempted to take the hat off and repeat the action. Instead, she remembered that there was no need to be rude —merely firm.

"I'm sorry, did I take your chair?" she said, still not looking up. "Or, perhaps, I'm in the way of your view?" Her tone wasn't exactly curt, but it was clipped and to the point.

"Nothing like that," he said. "But, if you were, I'd say you were entitled to it."

She rolled her eyes again and gave up the hope that he would go away. She should have expected this. A single woman with a book in her hands was supposed to be a clear signal: leave me alone. Apparently, this man had missed the sign.

"I'm sorry, but—" She looked up and stopped midsentence. Brice Simmons stood before her in all of his star-actor glory. He was tall, at least six feet, with broad shoulders, muscled arms and chest revealed beneath the deep V of his button-down Hawaiian print shirt, and a boyish grin that belied his forty years. To say he was tan was an understatement and it only helped to offset his bright white smile. The same smile women around the globe had lusted over for the last twenty years of his somewhat tumultuous career.

Margot closed her gaping mouth and tried to regain some of her composure. “Uh, what is it that you need of me then?”

*He’s just a man.* But even as she tried to convince herself of that, she found it difficult to keep her thoughts straight with the exceptionally handsome man towering over her.

“I was wondering if this seat is taken.” He indicated the lounge next to her in a row of five empty seats next to it. He was going to sit right next to her?

Her mouth went dry and her stomach clenched. She’d brought engaging reading because she wanted to be lost in the world of fiction, but not even one of her favorite authors could keep her distracted with Brice Simmons sitting next to her.

But that was ridiculous. She chided herself for her foolish, schoolgirl thoughts. She was a forty-one-year-old woman who owned a pastry shop. Not some teen with a star-crush looking for a ship romance.

“Sure,” she said, her voice sounding pinched in her own ears, “feel free.”

He grinned as if he sensed the underlying tension and the effect he had on her, then he slipped into the seat next to her. His long, muscled legs, just as tan as the rest of him, stretched out on the lounge. Then he began to unbutton his shirt.

She yanked her gaze back to her novel, feeling her cheeks heat, and desperately tried to read the rest of the first page. It was two short paragraphs but she kept reading the first line, hyper-aware of every move the man next to her made.

When he pushed the chair back a few clicks and laced his fingers behind his head, she let out a breath, closed her eyes for a few moments, then tried to refocus on the page.

"What are you reading?"

Heat rushed through her again. She knew she should tell him to mind his own business and get back to her book, but now the curiosity that was ingrained in her came to life. "David Baldacci's latest."

"He's good. Thrillers, huh?" His tone was conversational and her mind supplied an image of him in his latest action flick.

"Yep," she said, eyes still focused on the first page.

Finally, after several minutes, he spoke again. "My name's—"

"I know who you are," she interrupted then felt foolish.

"Then I'm at a disadvantage."

Relegating herself to the reality that she obviously wasn't

going to get any reading done, she closed her book, keeping her finger in her place, and looked over at Brice.

"Margot Durand." She leveled her gaze on him.

"Nice to meet you. Are you…traveling alone?"

The urge to roll her eyes was strong again, but she resisted. "In a way, yes."

His eyebrows rose above his dark sunglasses. "I'm not sure I know what that means."

Then she saw them walking across the deck. Two women in bikinis with light, see-through wraps draped over their impossibly fit bodies. They were, no doubt, heading this way.

"Well, I can see that *you're* obviously not traveling alone, so I'll just find another, *quieter*, area to read and let you have this extra chair. Looks like you'll need it." She forced a smile and stood, collecting her things just as the girls reached them.

"There you are, sweetie," one said, bending down to kiss him on the cheek, but he pushed her hand off his shoulder and sat up.

"You don't have to go. They aren't—"

"Who's this?" the other girl asked, her gaze hard on Margot.

"Really," he said, standing as she turned to walk away. "They aren't—"

"It's all right, Mr. Simmons. Your reputation precedes you."

And with that, she turned and left the handsome celebrity on the deck.

~

MARGOT FELT the heat of their exchange long after she had stepped into the coolness of the mezzanine area, but she would not be convinced by her fickle emotions. Sure, Brice Simmons was as handsome as they came and a talented actor too, but Margot was smarter than that. Smarter than to think his attention was anything other than a diversion to his otherwise planned out life. Wasn't that how most celebrities lived?

And then an image of Adam appeared in her mind and she smiled. Besides, when there was a man like Adam waiting for her back in Long Beach, and Virginia beyond that, Brice couldn't compare.

Pushing her tote further up on her shoulder, she trailed through the small shops and picked up a few small items for her friends back in North Bank. A crossword book with nautical terms for Bentley, a magnet for Rosie, and a postcard that she would send to the shop for them all. She intended to do more shopping in Ensenada, but for now, she enjoyed thinking of them as she shopped. A suitable gift for Dexter eluded her though.

Then she ordered a latte and sat down at one of the more

secluded tables on the main floor. Vibrant green plants sheltered her from those passing by and soon she was engrossed in the thriller that had proved so difficult to keep her focus on the deck. Occasionally sipping her coffee, she spent an hour reading before low voices broke into her concentration.

"I don't know. It's just what I heard."

"But…I didn't even know he was married," another voice replied, this one higher pitched and nasally, making Margot think of a mouse.

"Well, if it *is* true then she's going to know about it the minute we get back to Long Beach," the first voice said.

"What makes you say that?" Mouse said.

"For one, stuff like that doesn't just stay on the ship. And secondly, I mean—hello," the first woman paused for affect. "He's the captain. And if someone saw him with her…well, it's just going to get out. You'll see."

"That's so sad. I really liked her."

"Whatever. If she's messing up his marriage, it serves them both right."

The voices trailed off and Margot saw two crewmembers walk past. Finding it unsettling that she'd just been privy to a very private conversation about none other than the ship's captain, she closed her book and headed off to find Addie in the kitchen area.

Trying to shake off the sad thoughts of a man cheating on his wife, Margot nearly missed the entrance to the kitchen. She pressed the door open soundlessly but stopped just inside when she heard low but forceful voices. They were coming from the back of the kitchen, but she couldn't tell if it was Addie or not.

Then her friend's voice was clearly heard. "I just don't understand!"

Margot stepped forward, ready to go to her friend's aid, when she bumped into the metal prep table in the middle of the room and sent the spatulas, spoons, and other utensils clattering to the floor.

"I don't know how many times I've told you to—" Addie stopped when she saw Margot with her hands outstretched to pick up the utensils. "Oh, Margot. I thought you were Noah."

Margot offered a forced smile as she righted the canister at the same time she heard a door closing. So there was another way out of the kitchen.

"Is everything all right?" she asked, looking into her friend's eyes.

Addie avoided her direct gaze and fumbled with the edge of her apron. "Yeah. I'm just not…feeling well."

"Is there anything I can do?"

"For a headache?" Addie looked up, her wry smile unconvincing. "I don't think so. But thank you anyway."

She stepped back, untying her apron. “Hey, why don’t I meet you for dinner tonight at The Acapella Room? I’ll get us reservations and we’ll catch up then. I think I’m just going to get some rest now. If you can fend for yourself?”

Every intuition Margot had told her that her friend was lying, but she wasn’t sure that she should press the issue. Yet.

“All right, honey, you go on. I’ll meet you there tonight, okay?”

“Thank you,” Addie said, grabbing Margot’s hand and squeezing for a moment. “I’ll see you there tonight.”

Margot watched her go, her suspicions aroused. Something was definitely wrong with her friend, but she wasn’t sure what. And who had she been talking to in the backroom?

Her curiosity got the best of her and she made her way to the small office space at the back of the kitchen. There was another door. Margot opened it and popped her head into the hall, looking up and down it both ways. What corridor was this? She couldn’t be sure unless she reached the end of the hall where additional directions were usually posted, but she had checked the door handle and it was locked from the inside. Without a key, she’d be locked out and likely more than a little lost.

Instead, she pulled the door closed behind her and went back into the kitchen. She was about to leave when she heard the office door open. A moment later, Noah came into the room.

“Oh, Margot.” He stumbled back a few steps. “I didn’t know you’d be here.”

“I was just about to leave. I…” She fought for a good explanation but couldn’t find one. “Were you here earlier?”

He frowned. “Earlier? No.” He shook his head, looking genuinely confused. “I was, uh, making my rounds between the kitchens and our bakery shop in the mezzanine. Why? Did you need something?”

“No,” Margot was quick to reply. “Sounds like you’ve been busy.”

“I’m always busy. It’s the nature of the beast,” he said with a grin that didn’t quite meet his eyes.

“You said you’ve worked here three years?” she asked.

“Yes, but before that, I was on a few different cruise lines. I feel like I practically grew up on a boat.”

“Seems like it,” she mused. “Well, I’d better get going. I’m going to do a lap or two around the ship—I hear that’s great exercise.”

“It is,” he said, nodding with knowledge. “Enjoy it.”

She left the kitchen feeling his gaze on her back. He probably wondered what she was doing in the kitchen without Addie, but as soon as she’d asked if he had been there earlier, she felt as if she'd locked herself into a bit of a trap. Since Noah hadn't been the voice from earlier—or he hadn't admitted to it—then if she'd said she'd seen Addie, he'd know Addie had been there with someone. Maybe she was being paranoid, but on a ship that put so much stock in gossip, she wasn't going to risk her friend's reputation.

Shaking her head, she mentally berated herself. She was doing it again. Meddling. Poking her nose where it didn't belong. Why couldn't her friend have just had a disagreement? Those happened all the time. There was no need to read more into it.

Besides, she was on vacation. It was time to start acting like it.

# CHAPTER 4

Margot slipped on a long, cotton shift dress with tiny blue and white stripes. Accented with a golden anchor necklace and a lightweight grey cardigan, she slipped into her sandals and walked to dinner. The evening was cool, but not unpleasant, and she breathed in the salty air as she walked along the outside deck to reach The Acapella Room.

She'd read up on the menu and requested attire of this particular restaurant and looked forward to seeing the chef's creations. Her stomach growled in response and she secretly hoped that Addie was already there with their seat.

The walkway curved with the ship and, as she stepped past a young couple walking with their arms around one another, she caught a glimpse of a tall man in a dark blazer and jeans a hundred yards in front of her. What caught her attention were the jeans. They were distinctive

—a specific designer that liked to make flashy pockets on the back of all of his jeans—and she'd seen those jeans before.

Or, at least, she thought she had, on Gabe Williams.

But what would *Gabe* be doing on board a ship in the middle of the Pacific Ocean? Unless he was on a vacation, she reasoned. That was likely, seeing as he lived in Long Beach and he *had* said he would be busy this week and for Adam to call him the next week…but it seemed odd to her that he hadn't said anything about the cruise. She hadn't mentioned hers, but that was because she didn't know Gabe.

Frowning as she passed the hall that she needed to turn down, she took one glance in the direction of The Acapella Room and then kept walking. He appeared to be alone and in no hurry, but she followed at a discrete distance anyway. Still, she wasn't positive it was him. How could she explain following him if he turned around and found her standing there? Then again, she could have been going in the same direction as he was and then she'd play the surprised act about meeting a friend of a friend and what a small world it really was.

Could she pull that off though? Unlike Brice Simmons, she was no actress.

Up ahead, Maybe Gabe opened a door and slipped into the interior of the ship. After waiting a moment, she followed suit, hoping it wasn't going to be a long hallway with no place to hide, in case he turned around. But when she stepped inside the hallway, she was faced with an empty corridor in both directions.

Where had he gone? She hadn't even seen his face clearly enough to know if it really was Gabe either.

Feeling frustrated that she'd missed her opportunity, she was about to go back outside and make her way to dinner when she heard a door close down the hall to her left. Only after a moment's hesitation did she set off in that direction. She relaxed her shoulders and, rather than looking inquisitive, she tried to look like she was simply lost. That way, if Gabe did come around a corner or out of a room, she would be able to feign misunderstanding of directions. Though, if he were anything like Adam, he'd see right through that.

Why was she suspicious of him anyway? It was her nature to question and investigate, one of the things her late husband Julian had loved about her—or so he'd said. But it went back to his conversation with Adam at the restaurant and the fact that he looked as if he worked for a multimillion-dollar company, not the Long Beach police force. Or had she read into that? No, Adam had clearly said he was one of "Long Beach's finest," hadn't he?

The closer she came to what looked like a bend in the hall the more anxious she felt. Would she turn the hall and come face to face with him? Did he know she was following him? Was she being overly worried for no reason?

At the end of the hall, she read the sign that denoted what she would find if she turned in that direction. She was on the southeast wing, level five, or so the sign said. The arrow pointing around the corner indicated that it led to the sports equipment area. What did that mean?

Taking a risk, she did a quick peek around the corner to find the short hallway closed. Then the sound of something falling, muffled by the closed door, could clearly be heard. Someone was in the sports equipment room. But who? Maybe Gabe? And would they come back out this door? Her stomach clenched and she looked around. Aside from a very thin, very fake looking plant, and a door marked Housekeeping Closet, there was nowhere but back.

She heard another sound, this time something moving in the sports room followed by footsteps coming toward the door.

It was now or never. She was either going to pretend to be lost and risk whoever it was seeing through her cover, or she was going to…

Her gaze snagged on the housekeeping closet again and without thought, she pulled the door open. Thankful to see it was large enough to stand in, she stepped inside and closed the door, praying it wouldn't somehow be locked, not allowing her back out. Then she waited, holding her breath.

Moments later, she heard a door open then close and then

rapid footsteps heading back down the hall. Hoping to catch a glimpse of who it was, she went to open the door but it wouldn't move. Panic surged through her. Was she locked in to this small closet?

Taking in a steadying breath, she gripped the handle more firmly and shoved. The door burst open, taking her with it into the hall. Her first thought was relief at not being locked in the closet, but the second was whether or not she'd alerted whoever it was to her presence. She looked around and found that the halls were empty. It wasn't far back to the outside door, she reasoned, and the person had already made it outside.

Letting out a shaky breath, she closed the closet door and went toward the sports storage area. The door was closed, but when she tried the handle, it moved easily and opened out toward her. She stepped inside, the only lights that of an exit sign across the room and then the light flooding in from the hallway.

Margot pulled out her cellphone and tapped on the flashlight app, stepping inside the room but keeping the door open. She wasn't about to risk getting trapped in another room, even if only for a moment.

It looked like the room housed all sorts of sports equipment, hence its name, for guest's recreation while on board and probably even for when they docked in Mexico. In front of her she saw what must have fallen, alerting her to the person's presence in the room. A set of golf clubs lay on the ground, another set standing upright beside them.

She gingerly stepped over them then stopped, frozen in place. There, sticking out between a bin of beach balls and a wrapped up pool volleyball net, were a pair of ruby red high heels still attached to a pair of legs.

Slowly, careful not to disturb anything else, Margot stepped around the equipment and froze. It was a woman lying face down on the ground. She wasn't moving.

~

"YOU SAY YOU WERE LOST?"

Margot swallowed. She didn't like lying and made a habit not to, but in this instance, she wasn't sure it was appropriate, or in her best interests, to point out she was following a man that she thought to be a Long Beach police officer…and she hadn't actually seen him go into the room. She'd only heard someone.

"In a manner of speaking. I mean, there are so many halls on this ship." She gave a light laugh even though that felt wrong in the presence of a dead body.

"Right." The ship's lead security officer, Harvey Pearson, was a grizzled older man with weathered features she'd expect to see on a man who had fished for a living, but he assured her that he'd been a cop before taking his 'cushy gig' on board the *Carousel Luxury*.

"And was it exactly that drew you to come into the sports storage facility?" His eyebrows rose at the question but she didn't feel as if he doubted her story, only that he was trying to understand it.

"I heard someone in there and then the sound of something falling. I assume it was those clubs." She indicated the fallen golf clubs.

"And you didn't see anyone?"

"No." She flushed and looked down. "I actually stepped into the, um, housekeeping closet."

His eyebrows shot up even higher. "And may I ask why?"

"I felt foolish," she said, embellishing on one of her feelings, even if it wasn't the main reason. "I mean, I was lost at the end of a hall and..." She shrugged.

He pursed his lips. "Look, if there's something you aren't telling me—"

Just then the door opened and a tall, handsome man strode in. He wore a navy blue jacket with gold braiding indicating he was the captain. Margot assessed him, her mind flitting to what she'd overheard that very day. He was good looking, probably in his early forties—maybe late thirties—and had a commanding presence about him. Then again, she knew she wouldn't be able to *see* unfaithfulness on a man. Though sometimes...

"Pearson, what is going on?" he said. His manner was

direct, if not a little gruff, and his voice reminded her of something but she wasn't sure what.

"Drugs. Looks like we've got an overdose."

The captain sighed. "Not again."

Margot's eyebrows shot up. "Again?"

"I'm sorry," the captain said, looking down at her. "Who are you?"

"I'm Margot Durand—"

"The pastry chef?"

She was surprised the captain knew about her presence on board with hundreds of staff to account for. "Um, yes."

"Pleased to meet you. I'm Captain Grayson Haus. And what exactly are you doing here? You're a long way from the kitchen."

"I was the one who found the…body."

He looked to the side where two of Harvey's coworkers were documenting everything. "Right. Well, I am terribly sorry for you. This is supposed to be a vacation and…" His eyes narrowed. "You're awfully calm about all of this."

"I was thinking the same thing," Harvey said.

Margot shrugged. "My late husband was a detective and I've…seen my share of dead bodies. Unfortunately." Both men looked surprised but she pressed on. "You've had drug overdoses on board before?"

The captain looked around as if he was afraid of being overheard but something in his expression softened. "Look, Mrs. Durand, this cruise goes to Mexico almost every week and there is an unsavory side to every town past the boarder, especially Ensenada. We've had our fair share of issues with recreational drugs being brought on board, though we do everything in our power to make sure that doesn't happen. Though, we've never had an overdose that was fatal." He ran a hand across the back of his neck. "Look, it's late. Once Harvey here has everything he needs from you, why don't you go back to your cabin to rest. I'm sure this has been trying."

She appreciated the captain's understanding nature, but she was more concerned by the fact that there was a dead body. What would they do? Contact the authorities? It would likely be the FBI that would investigate the case since it was on international waters.

"What do you plan to do?" she said, looking between both men.

"Don't you worry about it," Harvey said. She could almost hear the added, 'little lady.' "I'll be in contact with the proper authorities."

Margot wanted to take a better look at the woman, but she also didn't want to raise Harvey's suspicions any more than she already had. One more question couldn't hurt though, could it?

"Who is she?"

Both men turned to look at her. It was the Grayson who spoke first. "She was our sports and recreation coordinator. Kristen Chambers."

Margot nodded. "I see." At least that explained why she was in the sports closet, but it didn't explain why she was wearing a tight—and short—miniskirt, red heels, and a sequined top. "Are crewmembers usually allowed to…party?"

This time it was Harvey who answered her. "We discourage some…um, *personal* interactions between the staff and our guests, but we do encourage our staff to mingle when possible. She was well within her rights as a staff member to have a night out, just not with *this* type of recreation."

Margot understood. "I see."

"I think I have all that I need for now, but I may need to question you further or have you speak with the proper authorities when we reach port back in Long Beach."

"Yes, of course." She had assumed as much, but she knew the difference in pace between that of a drug overdose and a murder. Was this the former, or the later?

# CHAPTER 5

MARGOT REACHED her cabin not long after she'd been released from the sports equipment storage area, though she had stopped to pick up a container of food to take back to her room. She'd also placed a call to Addie on the ship's phone, wondering if she was worried, but she hadn't reached her friend. She'd even stopped by her room but without an answer, Margot went back to her room.

Famished as she was, she placed the food on the small table and pulled out her iPad. It wasn't that she didn't trust Harvey and his security team, but if they were going to wait to contact the authorities until they were headed back to Long Beach, wouldn't evidence grow cold?

She paused, her fingers hovering over the small, attached keyboard. Evidence? Here she was treating this drug overdose as a murder—something Harvey didn't think it was.

Sighing, she rested her head on her hand, elbow propped on the tabletop. It wasn't that she *wanted* it to be a murder case so much as she was afraid that certain elements weren't lining up. Like the fact that she'd been following someone she believed to be a police officer only to find a dead woman where he'd lead her. Then again, she wasn't certain it *had* been Gabe—either at the end of that hall or even on board at all.

Adam's name glared back at her from the top of the email she'd started. Should she go through with it? Would he only worry? Then again, could she phrase her questions in such a way that he wouldn't be suspicious? Perhaps ask if he'd met up with Gabe? Likely not, he was a smart man, but just maybe...

Her fingers flew over the small, bluetooth keyboard and once she'd hit send, she leaned back. A picture of a large cake topped with éclairs and *religieuse* stared back at her. One of her monumental creations she'd done in her years of competing to be the best French pastry chef in the world. Or something like that.

A soft, memory-laden smile edged onto her lips but was soon replaced with the reality that a woman had died that night. Why? Was it as simple—and horrible—as a drug overdose? Or was it something else altogether?

Dressing in pajamas, Margot ate the now mildly warm dinner she'd taken with her and then climbed into bed. She was exhausted from the mental strain as much as from the reality that, yet again, she'd come across a dead body. Even on vacation she couldn't seem to get away from it. But that prodding at the back of her mind, the one that urged her to desire the truth in all circumstances, reared its curious head. It was the same reason she'd sought out the truth in both her niece's case and her friend Tamera's husband's case. The truth had to prevail, and if she could do anything to help that along, then she would.

POUNDING on her cabin door jerked her from fitful sleep and she stumbled out of bed, reaching the door as another fit of pounding began.

"Addie?" she said, looking at her through bleary eyes.

"I'm sorry, Marg, but I had to see you. Can I come in? I brought coffee."

The scent of bold French roast wafted out of the paper cup her friend was holding and, despite the restless night she'd had, Margot nodded and reached for the liquid caffeine.

"I just can't believe it," her friend said, hand going to her forehead as she paced the small space from the bed to the door then back again. "I mean, a woman is *dead*!"

Margot nodded, sipping the black coffee and grimacing when she burned her tongue. "I know. I was there."

"You were *what?*"

Margot frowned. "Don't you check your messages? I stood you up for dinner last night and then phoned to let you know I had been detained due to the—" She almost said murder. "—death."

"I... No."

Margot observed her friend through narrowed eyes. There were bags under her eyes and her hair was disheveled. In fact, it almost looked as if she hadn't gone to bed at all. She was also pacing again. Was she nervous?

"Addie, calm down." She reached her hand out toward the girl. "Come sit with me. Calm down. Did you know the woman?"

Addie shook her head, biting her lip before she answered. "Not really. I mean, I'm down in the kitchens almost all the time and don't have a chance to really do much recreation. I just— I guess I'm shocked."

"Of course, that's natural. How did you hear about it?"

"At a staff briefing this morning. It's so unorthodox. I mean, nothing like this has ever happened."

"Do you know anyone who knew the girl well?"

"Not really," she said. "I mean, from what I heard, there weren't a whole lot of people who *did* know her. Someone did say they'd seen her leave the club last night. I guess she was on her way to...I don't know, take the party to the next level?"

"But it was still so early," Margot mused.

"Right? I said as much, but one of the pursers in charge of that club said he saw her there often, never on duty or anything, so she was well within her rights as a crewmember to be there, but still…it *was* early."

"Was she ever seen with a man?"

Addie looked over at Margot with a confused expression. "What?"

"Sorry, I suppose you wouldn't know that. I was just wondering…maybe she 'partied' with someone on staff."

"Oh, that I wouldn't know." Addie looked down at the coffee held in her hands. "All of this is just too much right now."

Her friend's words alerted her to something deeper going on than just her upset over the dead crewmember.

"Addie," she said gently, "what's going on?"

Her friend looked up with wide eyes. "What do you mean?"

"You just seem out of sorts. Is there something I can help you with? It's a great thing to unburden yourself to a friend sometimes."

"Oh, uh, no." She shook her head and managed a feeble smile. "I'm fine. Really. I'm just…upset about all of this."

Margot had the distinct feeling that the girl wasn't telling her the truth, but she had no way to know if that was true or not. It also didn't feel like the right time to pressure her for a further explanation.

"I'd better get back to work. I'm just on a break. The pastries won't bake themselves as you well know, but thanks for listening to me."

"Of course. Do you need help this morning?"

"Absolutely not," Addie said with a stronger smile, "you're only on duty tonight. I hope you can get some relaxation time in. And I almost forgot to ask. Do you want to explore Ensenada today? I'll be done by early afternoon when we dock. I'd be happy to show you around."

"That sounds wonderful. Meet you in the mezzanine around one then?"

"Perfect. See you then."

"Oh," Margot called out to her friend. "Is it possible to see a list of passengers on board?"

The request shocked her friend and she rushed to find a reasonable explanation rather than admitting she wanted to see if Gabe Williams was listed as a passenger.

"I thought I saw Brice Simmons but I wanted to make sure before I made a fool out of myself asking for an autograph."

"Oh," Addie laughed, "well, there isn't guest access to it but I could check for you."

"No, that's fine. I'll take my chances."

Addie gave a little wave and disappeared out the door while Margot slumped back against the bed pillows. She felt bad about the fib she'd told her friend since she knew the egotistical man had indeed been Brice, but that also meant there was no way she could see the manifest. Well...no easy way at least. Maybe it was time she did a little digging of her own.

~

MARGOT DRESSED in white linen capris and a light blue tank top under a lightweight polka dot navy sweater. She tucked her canvas tote that would serve as her purse over her shoulder and headed out into the hall. She walked down the now familiar route to the mezzanine, but instead of veering off to the left and out the double glass doors that showcased the deep blue ocean waters, she walked down the steps and toward the customer service area.

It was still early, though not as early as she was used to waking up to get to the bakery, but that meant there was only one purser overseeing the computers. Thankfully, it was a woman. Her ruse would work with a man, but probably not as well. Margot had thought long and hard about what she was going to do and, when she stepped up to the waist-high desk, a computer monitor and keyboard the only things constituting the woman's work space, she put on a warm, slightly shy smile.

"Hello and good morning, ma'am. How may I help you?"

"Good morning. I have a question." She looked around, lowering her voice though no one was around. She bit her lip and did her best to look embarrassed. "There was this man last night…" Margot gave a girlish giggle. "He was the *sweetest*. I met him in the bar and he gave me his room number, we're going into Ensenada today, but I lost it somewhere between the bar and my own room." She looked sheepishly at the woman. "Is there any way to find out where he is?"

She pursed her lips and put on an apologetic look. "I'm so sorry, ma'am, but we're unable to give guests' room numbers."

"Oh, I completely understand but…" Margot huffed out a breath and played up her dejected look. "I *really* liked him and he was so respectful. That's rare these days. I don't need to see him exactly, but could you page him? Do you do things like that on the ship?"

The woman shook her head again. "No, we don't really page. Although…" She tilted her head. "I could leave a note for him and make sure he gets it before this afternoon." She smiled and Margot wondered if this was going to work.

"That might be all right," she said, trying to look hopeful.

"His name was Gabe. Gabe Williams." The woman clicked through her program and Margot added, "I think he's staying on the East deck. Fifth floor or something."

After a few more clicks, the woman shook her head. "I'm so sorry, ma'am, but there's no one here under that name."

Margot hid her dismay with surprise. "What? You mean he *lied* to me?"

The woman looked sympathetically at her. "I'm sorry."

"Figures I would meet a nice guy who wouldn't be that nice. Well, thank you so much for your help."

"Not a problem. Have a great day."

The woman's cheery farewell followed Margot through the mezzanine and out onto the deck as she made her way to The Acapella Room for breakfast. So she hadn't seen Gabe. Or, if it had been him, he was here under an assumed name. And she'd followed him to the room where a dead body had been found.

She was so preoccupied that she didn't even notice the handsome, tanned man blocking her path until she collided with his solid chest. Warm hands reached out and lightly cupped here elbows, setting her back on her feet.

Righted, she looked up into aqua eyes that rivaled the ocean outside the wall of windows that faced west.

"Margot Durand."

"Brice Simmons," she said, barely holding in her grimace.

His flashing white teeth told her he was more than happy to see her. "Let's have breakfast."

She didn't need—or want—his flirty attention. "That's all right. I'm sure you're busy. I'm..." She looked around for an excuse and spotted the two young women she'd seen the day before. This time they were wearing more than they had been on the deck, but only by a little.

"I won't take no for an answer. This way." He motioned for a waiter as the two women came toward him. "Tiffany, Haden, you're dismissed for the morning."

They nodded and turned away as if this happened often and Margot had a feeling it did. "Really, I'm fine eating alone."

"On a cruise? You already read alone, a waste of time if you ask me. Besides, you can go home and tell everyone you had breakfast with Brice Simmons." This arrogant smile nearly took all of the air from the room, or at least it felt that way.

Margot wanted to say that none of her friends would really care, but that wasn't fully true. She had a feeling Taylor would 'flip out,' as she was prone to say. But aside from her celebrity-crazy niece, no one else would care. If he'd been Frank Sinatra, it might have been another story.

Resigning herself that it was either breakfast with Brice or going hungry, she listened to her stomach and followed him as the waiter showed them to a table.

"Glad you decided to join me," he said, flashing her a brilliant smile before ordering a coffee with more qualifiers than Margot thought possible.

She ordered coffee with cream and then turned her gaze on the man sitting across from her. "You hardly gave me a choice."

There was that grin again. "Well, you looked lonely standing there. Besides, what I said was right, you can't go on a cruise by yourself."

She hiked an eyebrow. "You can, and I did."

"And how much fun are you having?"

"Actually…" She looked to the side, thinking of the body she'd found last night. "Not that much fun, but that's no fault of the cruise or being alone."

His gaze narrowed. "Are you talking about the body you found?"

"How did you know about that?" She was genuinely shocked.

"Oh, my staff likes to share information with me."

"Your staff?"

"Tiffany and Haden. They are my assistants."

They certainly didn't dress like any assistants Margot had ever seen. "Still, how did they know about it?"

"It's their job to be informed."

"I'd say that's more than staying informed."

"Think of it this way, if there's a threat that could affect me, it's their job to know."

That was interesting. The women looked like two pieces of arm candy, but she knew better than to categorize people by how they looked.

"They are your security?"

"That's Haden," he said with a grin, "Tiffany is my personal assistant."

"Interesting."

He leaned his elbows on the table. "I know it's unorthodox, but Haden graduated top of her class at the police academy and, once she'd had enough of being a public servant, she sought out something a little more profitable."

Everything about that statement made Margot recoil.

"What?" Brice said as their food arrived. He had insisted on ordering instead of choosing the buffet option and Margot had to admit the steaming bowl of oatmeal with artfully placed fruit on top did looked amazing. "I can tell something I said made you unhappy."

"My husband—my *late* husband," she added when she saw his surprised look, "was one of those odious 'public servants'."

"And you don't like that she wanted to make enough money to pay off her school debts?"

Margot narrowed her eyes. "I take no issue with that."

"You said late. How did your husband die?"

His question shocked her and she almost choked on the bite of oatmeal she'd just taken. "You don't pull any punches," she observed.

"Sorry," he said, shrugging. "I've found that I can come across rather abruptly at times. I suppose it's just a fault I have."

That, or it was the reality that he could get away with asking whatever he wanted, whenever he wanted, due to his celebrity standing. Either way, she wasn't sure she wanted to open up about her husband's death with this total stranger.

"I only ask," he continued, popping a grape into his mouth and chewing thoughtfully for a moment, "because I've experienced loss as well."

Her eyebrows rose and she took a breath. What she would share with him wouldn't be anything more than what she'd share with anyone else. "My husband was a detective in our small town in Virginia. He was a casualty during a particularly dangerous case he was working. A wrong place, wrong time sort of thing."

"Oh, Margot," Brice said, reaching across the table and resting his hand over hers, "I'm so sorry."

She smiled but gently pulled her hand away. "It was five years ago. The wounds, though painful, aren't as fresh as they once were."

Brice didn't seem to notice her withdrawal and kept his hand on her side of the table as his vibrant blue eyes poured into hers. "My sister died of a drug overdose."

"I'm sorry to hear that," she said, genuinely sorry for him.

"It was terrible," he said, leaning back and shaking his head, lost in his own thoughts. "I can still remember what I was doing when I heard the news. Drugs. Terrible things."

Margot narrowed her eyes, trying to understand the enigma in front of her. He was gregarious, handsome, and charming, but there was something underneath all of that that Margot couldn't quite point out. A feeling. Something like an underlying current that felt off. Perhaps that was what celebrity did to a person.

They finished up their breakfast, the conversation remaining light and mostly revolving around Brice's considerable knowledge of Mexico. When Margot was done, she pushed her plate forward, took the last sip of her coffee, and made her excuses to leave.

"You're welcome to join us in Ensenada if you'd like. We'll be having a lot of fun." He grinned and winked.

"Thanks, but I've got plans. Thanks again for breakfast."

He merely grinned and she felt his eyes on her as she left the dining room. It had been the strangest breakfast she'd ever had.

# CHAPTER 6

MARGOT WAS MARVELING at the incredible view when she rounded the corner and ran into Noah. Blinking rapidly in surprise, she stepped back but immediately noticed the young man's expression. Was it sorrow or anger?

"Noah, are you all right?"

He stiffened when he saw her and his expression changed to one of sadness. "I'm sorry... I just...sorry."

"Did you know the woman who died?" She blurted it out before she could couch her speech, but the words seemed to shock him out of his stupor.

"Yeah." His jaw clenched. "I knew Kristen."

Margot studied his expression, but he turned his gaze out toward the ocean. "I heard she was new to the ship?" She wasn't sure why she was asking exactly, but it did seem odd that the young man, who had been on the ship for three years, would know a new crewmember despite the fact that he was so busy working in the kitchens. Was he known to attend the clubs? Was that where they'd met? Or had they known one another off of the ship?

"I didn't know her all that well," he was quick to explain. "We'd just gotten drinks a few times off ship. You know. Caught up in Ensenada and did some touristy things together." He snuck a glance at Margot and forced a tightlipped smile.

"I'm so sorry to hear that she passed away as she did."

His eyes narrowed, "How did you hear about it?"

"I discovered the body."

"You did?" He looked completely shocked, but she also noticed that his face paled, the color all but draining from his features.

"Yes." She wrapped her arms around herself as the breeze picked up. She could just make out land in the distance and knew that within an hour, they would be docked in Ensenada.

"Yeah, and to overdose like that…" He shook his head and his expression hardened. "Pretty dumb if you ask me. But I've got to get going. Sorry."

"Oh, yes of course." She took a step back. "I'll see you tonight?"

He frowned. "Tonight. Right. Yeah, see you then."

She watched him walk away, surprised at the change in his demeanor. If Addie barely knew the young recreation staffer, how had Noah met her? Were they closer than he'd let on?

Pushing her inquisitive desire to the side, she went to the deck and took up a spot on an empty chaise lounge, planning on reading until they pulled into port. At least while she was here she wouldn't be tempted to look into the mysterious death of the young woman.

Then again, it wasn't *that* mysterious. Many people overdosed from drugs. It happened...but still, it bothered Margot for more than just the obvious reasons. The young woman had been dressed for a party, and yet she'd overdosed in the sports equipment room without anyone around. That didn't make sense.

Then a thought occurred to Margot. She put her book away and pushed off the lounge. Taking her cue from the sounds of shouting and cheering on the other side of the deck, she walked toward the recreation area.

Standing on the sidelines, she watched the organized game of pool volleyball. There were two crewmembers, a young woman and a young man. They both looked happy and enthusiastic with their job and the woman was cheering loudly for the players in the pool. The young man commented something to the woman and picked up a bag that looked like it was full of equipment and started heading toward the door leading inside.

This was her chance. Margot circumvented the crowd on the deck watching the volleyball game and met up with the young man just before he went inside.

"Excuse me," she said, putting on a warm smile. "I was wondering if I could ask you a question."

He looked surprised that she'd stopped him but characteristic of all of the crewmembers that she'd interacted with, he was only happy to oblige. "Yes, ma'am, how can I help you?"

"I know this may seem…unorthodox but…" She managed to look uneasy. "I was the woman who found…Kristen Chambers."

The young man's expression changed to one of shock and sorrow. "Oh, I'm so sorry to hear that. It's a terrible thing that happened."

She nodded, agreeing. "I just…I guess I wanted to know more about her. Maybe that sounds odd to you, but I just can't get that image out of my mind and I thought that, maybe if I knew more about her, I could…you know, move on?"

"Oh, I understand," he said, nodding. A look of sympathy overtook his handsome features.

"I was just curious about what kind of woman she was?" Margot schooled her features, looking interested but not *too* interested.

"She was great. Really good at her job. I know that

passengers really seemed to love her." His expression fell and he looked appropriately sad. "To be honest, I didn't know her well."

"Why not?" Margot looked openly curious.

"We worked different shifts pretty much consistently and she was new. I hadn't seen her around much so..." He shrugged to emphasize his point.

"Yeah, that makes sense." Margot scrunched up her nose. "So you never saw her...out? I mean, the heels and outfit she had on last night were pretty fancy."

"You could ask Carol over there. I know she likes to visit some of the clubs on board. She might know."

"Thanks so much," Margot said, offering him a warm smile, which he returned before heading inside.

Margot stood to the side and watched the game wrapping up. She still had an hour or more before she would need to meet Addie for their jaunt into town and she still had questions about Kristen. She was apparently liked by all but not really known by many—except for Noah. Had he met her at a club? If so, would Carol know?

When the game broke up, Margot watched as the woman collected the volleyball items and told everyone when they could expect the next tournament. She hauled a cloth bag with the balls and the netting from across the pool toward the same door that the young man had gone through.

"Hello," she said with a friendly smile when she approached the door where Margot still stood. "Can I help you?"

"Well." Margot again looked sheepish. "I was wondering if I could ask you a few questions…about Kristen Chambers."

The name shocked the woman but her smile only faltered slightly. "What type of questions? And, if I can ask, why are *you* asking them of me?" She asked in a kind, respectful way that Margot appreciated.

Margot explained how she had found the woman and that she was just trying to make sense of it all and get to know a little more about the woman whose life had ended. Just as the young man had, Carol softened immediately.

"I'm sorry you had to go through that—and on a vacation no less." She shook her head.

"Did you know Kristen then? The other young man who was helping you seemed to think you might know her better than he did."

Carol shrugged. "Well, maybe. She hadn't been with us very long and I really hadn't gotten a chance to get to know her well. I did see her at one of the clubs, though. In fact, it wasn't last night but the night before."

"Really? I noticed last night—" Margot grimaced. "—that she was dressed to go out."

"Yeah, I could tell right away she was a regular party girl.

Was dancing with this one guy. They seemed to really hit it off."

Margot's mind filled in the blank. "Was he tall and blonde? Good looking?"

"No," she said, shaking her head. "Tall, but he had dark brown hair, kind of curly I think? Looked like he was wearing some pretty expensive jeans. I know, terrible thing to notice, but that fancy stuff on the pockets sticks out."

Margot felt the breath leave her lungs. Jeans with fancy pockets. Gabe?

"Yeah, I know exactly what you mean."

"Sorry, but we really didn't talk much. She bunked with a few other women but I didn't see her around a lot. She kind of kept to herself when she wasn't on duty."

Margot nodded and thanked the woman. The new information filled her mind with questions. If the man in question dancing with Kristen *was* Gabe, how did they know one another? Did they even know one another? And was it a coincidence that Margot had been following who she thought was Gabe only to find Kristen dead?

The questions stacked up against one another but the timer on her phone went off, alerting her to the fact that it was time to make her way to the mezzanine to meet Addie. The questions would have to wait.

~

MARGOT ALMOST MADE a grave mistake as she made her way to the appointed meeting area. She almost ran into Brice. But, at the last minute, she slipped behind a large bank of leafy plants, sucking in a breath at how close it had been. He was a nice man, she'd give him that, but he was self-assured, arrogant, and no doubt wanted her to join him in exploring Ensenada. Something she wasn't going to do. Sure, she could turn him down, but when she'd tried that at breakfast it hadn't gotten her far.

Now, as she stood breathing shallowly so as not to draw any attention her way, she ground her teeth realizing that Brice and his *associates* had stopped just on the other side of her hiding spot.

"And you're absolutely sure, Haden? I mean we're talking about murder here."

Margot pressed her lips together so firmly she felt her teeth leaving impressions on the inside. Had he just said *murder*? It only made sense that he was talking about Kristen, but as far as she knew, it was an overdose. A sweet girl who'd partied too hard.

Still, that explanation hadn't sat well with Margot anyway.

"I'm telling you there's no connection. We're clean. But we have to go. He called."

The voice of one of his assistants was low but easy

enough for Margot to hear. So they had knowledge of the crime? What did this mean? And what did she mean they were clean? And who had called? How was Brice, of all people, involved with any of this? Or was he? Had Kristen known him or approached him at the club perhaps? That sounded like a place that Brice might go at night on the cruise ship.

It was all a big guess, though. There was no way for her to know more information...unless...

The sound of Brice and his assistants walking away drew Margot's attention. She checked the time and saw that Addie was already fifteen minutes late. Biting her lip, Margot surveyed the mezzanine. Not seeing her friend, she made a hasty decision. She left a note at the customer help desk, hoping that Addie would get it, and went in search of the handsome and potentially devious celebrity.

She rushed to the railing of the boat and looked out to the gangplank. Near the exit, she spotted Brice and his two female assistants. She'd have to hurry, but maybe she could still catch up with them and gain an invitation to tour the city with them as Brice had offered before.

Holding onto her canvas tote, she rushed down the steep slope toward the dock, careful not to let her sandals slide. At the dock, she skirted past disembarking passengers. The crowds were thinning, though there were still plenty of people around. Taxis lined up, their drivers waving their hands and speaking in broken English to attract any customer they could.

Brice stopped near one such taxi and she seized her chance. Trying not to look or sounded winded, Margot smoothed her hair and stepped up toward him.

"Hello, Brice," she said with a smile.

"Margot, fancy seeing you here." His smile was bright but there was something holding it back. Was it his thoughts of murder?

"Is your offer still valid for a little tour of Ensenada? I find myself with a free afternoon."

Now his smile definitely slipped. "Oh, I'm so sorry. You'd said you were busy and...well, something's come up. I won't be able to show you around today."

Odd. For someone who had seemed intent on having her join him, he'd sure changed his tune quickly.

"Oh really? You can't spare any time?" She fluttered her eyelashes, nearly making herself sick as she did.

"I'm really sorry." He widened his eyes trying to express the truth of his regret. His hand slipped to her arm. "Any other time..." He looked away as another car pulled up. It wasn't a taxi but an expensive black car. The driver got out and he was wearing a dark suit and white shirt. He opened the door and said, "Mr. Simmons?"

"Come on, Brice," the woman with blonde hair said. "Sorry." She flashed a fake smile at Margot that gave her the distinct impression she wasn't sorry at all, then ushered her boss toward the car, his hand sliding from Margot's arm.

"Rain check?" he said, a hopeful light coming into his eyes.

Margot said nothing and watched as he slid into the dark interior, one of the assistants with him and the other into the front seat.

She watched as they pulled slowly into traffic. The urge to follow him was so strong that Margot didn't even try to ignore it. She found the next available taxi and nodded to him. "Let's go."

The man, short with a dark moustache, grinned and hopped into the front seat. "*Si, Senora.* Where to?"

His English was better than she'd expected, but for a tourist town, she knew she shouldn't be too surprised. "Can you follow that town car?"

She pointed ahead to the black car and the man turned to look at her. "Follow?"

How was she going to explain this?

"Is he...you know, your lover?"

"Uh..." She bit her lip.

"I got it. *Silencio.*" He grinned and swerved into traffic despite the blaring horns of those behind him.

Margot slumped back into the worn leather interior of the older car. She knew this wasn't the brightest idea she'd had. Even as she thought it, she heard Adam's voice in her head berating her for taking a chance like this. Then again, she was in a cab. She was just following the man to see where he went in a city he seemed immensely knowledgeable of. If it looked like they were driving into a bad part of town, she'd have—

Frowning, she peered up at the name on the dash. It said Juan. Well, then she'd have Juan turn around and take her somewhere in town where she could do some sightseeing. A stab of guilt struck her as she thought about Addie. She had come on this cruise as a favor to her friend but also to spend time with the woman. Then again, it seemed Addie had things she needed to attend to that had kept them apart as well, but still… Should she have stayed around and waited for her friend rather than follow Brice?

Just then Juan pulled over.

"Why are we stopping?"

"They stop. You stop. *Si?*"

"Yes. *Si.*" She peered up ahead and saw Brice and the two women get out of the car. They were on a side street but she'd noticed the larger main thoroughfare a few streets over. They were still in what appeared to be a good neighborhood and Margot knew if she got out here, she was only a few blocks' walking distance to touristy crowds and shops.

"Thank you, Juan," she said, tossing a 500-peso bill at him.

He grinned, appreciating the tip. "You need me to wait?"

She shook her head. She wasn't planning on crashing his party, but she did want to see what was so important that Brice would rescind his offer. Not that she was such an important person to him, but he'd made it clear he wanted her company that day but something had definitely changed.

"*Adios*," Juan said, then drove off.

Stepping into the shade of a nearby building, she donned a floppy hat she'd kept in her tote, shoving her shoulder-length hair up into the hat and leaving her neck and shoulders bare. Then she put on a large pair of sunglasses that hid a good portion of her face. And, for good measure, she took off her sweater and shoved it in her tote, which she carried by the straps instead of over her shoulder. It wasn't a great disguise, but she also didn't look like she had when she'd seen Brice last.

Then she strolled along the street, happy to see others walking around at a similar pace. When she got to the front of the building, she saw that it was a restaurant with a patio space out back. Rather than go in, she circled around to the back through a narrow alleyway just past the building. From there, she peeked out and could just see Brice and his assistants sitting down at a large table near a rock fountain.

The man seated at the table with them wore a blazer of a light blue, his pinstriped shirt opened much too low in the front to reveal gold chains mingling with his dark chest hair. His black-rimmed glasses gave him a distinguished, expensive look.

Who was this man? Why was Brice meeting with him? It obviously was important enough that he blew her off or couldn't take her with him. But more than that, she wanted to know what they were saying.

That was when she saw her opportunity. A mariachi band was making the rounds singing at each table and they had just finished up a song. They were coming toward the table that Brice was at and everyone's attention as on the band.

She took a breath and prayed for invisibility even as she jetted out toward the waterfall.

"Hey!" a voice cried out.

# CHAPTER 7

"PLAY SOMEWHERE ELSE!" the voice said.

Margot stood with her back plastered to the large rock waterfall structure that sat at the corner of the patio. There were tall palm trees jutting up into the sky, which provided natural shade but the water also acted as a cooling agent under the hot Ensenada sun.

She held her hand over her abdomen, her heart still pounding. She'd assumed they'd seen her make a dash for the relative cover of the waterfall, but apparently she had gone unnoticed while Gold Chain told off the mariachi band.

"I'm glad you could meet on such short notice," the man said.

Margot tried to move closer but was afraid of being seen, despite the lush foliage covering the rocks. The rushing water created a barrier to the sound and it was difficult to hear everything being said.

"I didn't feel like I had a choice." Brice's tone was clipped.

"Life is full of choices," the man said. His words were followed by a raspy laugh.

"Choices to cheat me?" Brice said.

"Cheat? What? What is this cheat?" Gold Chain sounded incredulous.

"I've given you what you asked for and you've consistently under-delivered."

"You don't know what you speak of, I—"

One of the women with Brice interrupted Gold Chain's tirade and said something but her tone was so soft that Margot missed it.

"Well, that is a lie. All of it is a lie. I had no hand in it. You come down here on your fancy cruise or shooting a movie and you think we are all barbarians. That's not how I do business." Gold Chain sounded angry now.

"We shall see," Brice said, sounding unconvinced.

Margot frowned. What was going on? What was Brice involved in and what had the man under-delivered on?

The woman was speaking again and Margot kicked herself. She knew if she moved any closer she would give away her position.

"Down to business—if you still wish to partner with me," Gold Chain finally said. His tone held anger but Brice didn't interrupt again. "I'm sending Andres here to run a very important errand, one you know that is very crucial to our...business. And we're going to have a Mexican feast. No more talk of cheating or murder."

So one of the women had mentioned the death on the ship—the *murder*. This filled Margot with curiosity, but she also honed in on the man's words. Who was Andres? If he was the one doing their bidding, then she needed to follow him. Especially if they were just going to sit and eat all afternoon.

Sending someone to do their bidding would make complete sense. Brice, though American, was still a well-known actor. If he'd shot a movie in Mexico as well, then more than just tourists could recognize him. There was no way he could be tied to...

Her thoughts came to a skittering halt. What? What *was* all of this?

"Andres, *llevar esto a* Ramone, *por favor*."

Risking a peek, Margot snatched a glance of Andres. He was tall, lanky, and dressed in a faded brown t-shirt with dirty khaki pants. He almost didn't look like he belonged in the restaurant, but she watched as he took the proffered envelope from Gold Chain and shoved it into his waistband at the front of his pants. No risk of pickpocketing that way.

She ducked back down behind the rocks when he turned to leave and contemplated her exit. There was no more mariachi band for her to count on for distraction. She glanced around and her gaze alighted on a large, black cord. Smiling to herself, she waited only a moment before yanking the cord.

Suddenly, the large fountain dripped to a stop. As expected, Gold Chain made a fuss at the fact that the cooling water had stopped and, seeing her opportunity, Margot slipped past the table that was focused on a harried waiter coming to the loud, jarring calls of the demanding man.

Smiling to herself, she slipped back down the alley and out toward the front of the restaurant just in time to see Andres at the end of the block. Thanking God that she'd worn comfortable sandals, she picked up her pace and reached the end of the block just in time to see Andres turn down a narrow alleyway. She was careful to keep her distance, and thankful that there were enough pedestrians to hide behind when Andres did a cursory glance behind him.

He stepped from the alley into the street and, after a few moments, she did the same. They had passed what she assumed was the main thoroughfare and were now on another side street. The dilapidated condition of the buildings made her stomach clench in unease but she kept on.

Then, as the foot traffic began to dissipate, Margot began

to worry that he would notice her. How could he not? She was a white, obviously American woman and stuck out like a store thumb. She hid behind a stack of old crates as he rounded another corner then came out just as two young men stepped into her path.

"*Hola, chica,*" one said with a sly smile.

She came to a halt and clasped the straps of her purse. She should have known better. The minute he left the more heavily populated areas, she should have gone back. But it was too late for 'should haves' and time for her to figure out her next move.

"Excuse me," she said and tried to walk around them.

"Hold on. Not so fast." The other one spoke and put a hand on her arm.

She immediately stepped back and sized them up. She had reached the Black Belt Level in Krav Maga and was confident of her ability, but she really didn't want to fight these men.

"Let me pass," she said, looking both of the men in the eyes.

"No." He reached out and went to grab for her, but she maneuvered past his grip with lightning speed.

The other man laughed at his buddy's inability to get a hold of Margot but she was already prepared for his attempt when a hand clamped down on her shoulder.

"There you are, honey," the voice said. Her stomach lurched and her attention jerked to the side to see who had come up behind her. Her shock nearly made her gasp.

*Gabe.*

She swallowed, blinking up at him. "These fellows weren't bothering you, were they?" He looked between the young men who started to back up when he appeared, seemingly out of nowhere.

"Nah, mister," one said, then they both turned and ran off.

"Honey?" she said, looking up at him, a million questions vying for her attention.

"I figured it was better than any other line I could come up with. Fancy meeting you here…Margot."

"Same to you, Gabe Williams."

"You've got a good memory."

"You've got good timing."

He gave her a cocky half-smile and shrugged. "What say we got back to the nicer parts of Ensenada?"

She agreed and let him lead the way. He seemed to know exactly where he was going and, when they reached the busy streets, he stopped near a vendor that sold fruit juice. Passing the woman a few pesos, he handed Margot a cold drink.

"Here, this'll help take the edge off."

She resented the fact that he thought he knew her, but she accepted the drink anyway and took a long sip. It was good.

"Are you on the cruise?" she asked, her eyes never leaving his face.

"I am."

"Do you know Kristen Chambers?"

He hesitated a moment too long, his weight shifting from one foot to the other, before he said, "That name doesn't ring a bell."

He was lying, but she had no way to prove that. Though she did think she caught a hint of something that passed behind his eyes. It was there and gone so fast she couldn't be sure, but it looked like sadness.

"Well, I trust you'll be all right to get back to the ship."

"I never asked you how you found me?"

He grinned. "Just lucky, I guess."

A loud noise drew her attention down the street and when she turned back, he was gone.

RATHER THAN CHANCE another unpleasant encounter with young men looking to scare foolish tourists who'd lost their way, Margot took another taxi back to the ship. She was cutting it close as it was and rushed to her room to change into her baking attire. Then she made her way to the kitchen.

When she arrived, she recognized Michael Bowers there, directing two burly Mexican men hauling in crates.

"Oh, Mrs. Durand," Michael said, his smile looking tight. "I didn't know you'd be here. I hope we're not disturbing you."

"No, I just came to get a head start on the desserts for the gala tonight."

"Ah yes," he said, looking down at his clipboard. "And Miss Petit?"

"I'm not sure where she is. She'll probably be along soon."

"Good." His curt reply matched his tight nod. "Just a delivery of flour. The workers will be gone any minute now."

Soon, the men had left and Michael gave her a slight bow before leaving as well.

Faced with a quiet kitchen, Margot let her mind wander. She needed the calming effect baking would have on her and was happy to get started without Addie, but her mind wouldn't let go of the strange events of the day. Where had Andres gone? Were the young men associated with him or were they just opportunistic? Where had Gabe come from? Had he been following Andres as well?

So many questions and yet nowhere near enough answers.

Rather than muddle through it all, she opened one door of the gigantic refrigerator and pulled out butter. Butter was always the perfect start to any recipe.

And then she set to work.

When Addie came in an hour later, she took in the work Margot had already done with surprise. "You've been busy."

Margot looked up and smiled. "Thought I'd make up for leaving you earlier today."

"Leaving me?" Addie tugged an apron on then turned to wash up at the sink. "What do you mean?"

"We were supposed to go into Ensenada today."

"Oh my gosh." Addie turned around, hands still dripping. "We *were*, weren't we?"

Margot was shocked. They had only made plans that morning and the girl had already forgotten? What was going on? She had never been so forgetful in school, Margot knew that for a fact. She appeared flustered and after the argument Margot had overheard, she wondered if there wasn't something seriously wrong going on.

"Addie," Margot said, resting her hands on the cool metal top of the counter. "What's going on?"

"Wh-what?" she said, toweling off her hands and turning

to the list Margot had made on the white board next to the bank of ovens.

“I’ve known you for years now and, though we haven’t seen each other much of late, I know you’re not some flighty school girl who forgets things like trips into town with her friend. Something’s got you preoccupied and I wish you’d just open up to me about it.”

“You’re right,” she said, her tone clipped. “I'm not *some school girl* and if there is anything wrong, it’s *my* business, not yours. You’ve always been nosy, Margot, but seriously —cut it out.”

Margot blinked, taken aback by the girl’s cruel words. Then, an instant later, Addie’s eyes welled with tears.

“I’m sorry—I didn’t mean that.” She let out a long breath and propped her hand on her hip, shaking her head. “I’m…I’m just under a lot of stress right now. And yes, there are some things that I really can’t share with you right now. Not with anyone really…” She looked over her shoulder as if someone would come in the door at that exact moment. “But I’ll tell you when I can, okay?”

Margot felt her sympathies return and nodded with a small smile. “Addie, I wouldn’t force you to tell me anything you didn’t want to. I just want you to know that I’m here for you no matter what. If you need a listening ear, okay. If not, that’s just fine.”

Addie held her gaze as if assessing if Margot really meant

what she said. Then, finally seeing what she needed to, she nodded. "All right."

"What do you say we make some amazing French pastries?"

Addie gave her a small smile, agreed with a nod, and they went to work. Halfway through their list of baked goods, Noah showed up. His face was red and splotchy as if he'd gotten a sunburned from being outside for too long, and he looked tired.

"Sorry," he said, slipping on his own apron. "I overslept on the beach."

Margot narrowed her eyes and noticed the line at the back of his neck. There was white skin next to beet red skin as if he'd gotten sunburned from above. That didn't usually happen on the beach since most men didn't wear shirts when they were lying out. Then again, maybe Noah did. Still, to be late to one of the most important baking times seemed extremely irresponsible.

He stepped to the whiteboard. "Want me to update?"

Addie gave a curt nod, no doubt unhappy at his tardiness, and went back to the dough she was working with. Margot watched as Noah took inventory of what they'd already gotten done and what was left to finish up. He put lines through the pastries they'd finished, wiped out a few pastries, and reorganized based on baking times. His writing was extremely neat and Margot smiled to herself thinking of Dexter and his chicken scratch.

When they were finally finished, Margot was shocked to see that they only had an hour until the gala was set to begin.

"You'll have enough time to get ready, right?" Addie asked, looking worried.

"Yes, of course." Margot took off her apron and tossed it on top of Addie's and Noah's in the bin near the back door. "I'll see you there?"

"Definitely. And Margot—" Addie stepped toward her. "I'm really sorry. About earlier. I…I was way out of line. You have always been a good friend to me and this— Well, it's killing me, but I really can't talk about it. Yet."

Margot wrapped her arms around her friend and squeezed lightly. "It'll be fine. And apology accepted. Now go get ready and I'll see you at the pastry table."

"Deal."

Margot watched Addie disappear into the back hall and turned toward the hall that would lead to her quarters. There was definitely something that Addie was hiding. Until this point, she hadn't considered it had anything to do with Kristen Chambers's death, but was she wrong to rule out her friend because she knew her?

Of course Margot didn't think Addie capable of murder, but that shouldn't negate the fact that her friend was definitely hiding something.

The only question was: what was she not telling Margot?

# CHAPTER 8

MARGOT HASTILY SWIPED SPARKLING eye shadow across her eyelids, biting her lip in the process and worried that she wouldn't be ready in time. The baking had taken longer than she expected, but she wasn't usually the type of woman to spend an exorbitant amount of time on her appearance. Instead, she did what she could to make her eyes pop with thicker eyeliner and an extra coat of mascara, and then she slipped into the sapphire blue dress she'd purchased just for this cruise. A woman had to treat herself every once in a while, didn't she?

After stepping into a pair of three inch, navy blue heels, she looked at herself in the full-length mirror on the back of the door. The dress hugged her curves and flowed out at the bottom in a mermaid style, and the sweetheart neckline sparkled with tiny, silver speckles that glittered in the overhead lights from the cabin. She felt elegant and allowed a small, ruby-lipped smile before turning to her iPad to check her emails before she left for the gala.

The smile appeared again when she saw that Adam had emailed her back. She immediately clicked on it and read his short reply. He told her not to worry and then wished her an exceptionally fun night, making sure to tell her that he hoped it would be full of surprises. Then, before the sign-off, he said he hoped she was wearing his favorite dress. She laughed out loud at this and shook her head, envisioning the dress he was talking about.

After they had attended the rainy Washington D.C. street festival, Adam had come to her pleading for her to join him at a fancy dinner to be held in D.C. He'd explained that his brother Anthony, a detective in D.C., had invited him and he needed to bring a plus one. He'd begged her, fighting off her halfhearted excuses with his charming smile, and she'd caved.

It was that night that she'd worn her fancy red dress, the one that had left Adam speechless for a full minute when he'd first seen her, and the same dress that had caused him to be distracted more than once during the party. She remembered his sweet smile even now.

Well, he wouldn't know it, but she had a feeling he'd like this blue dress just as much as the red.

She closed the case of the iPad and looked once more in the mirror before stepping toward the door. But then she hesitated. She wished Adam was there. He wouldn't stop until Kristen's death was properly investigated. He would have gone with her to trail the man. He would have— No, what was she thinking? He would have given her a stern talking-to if he even knew she'd gone out of the tourist safe zones in the city.

But there was one thing Adam definitely would have known—why Gabe Williams was on the cruise. Odd that he hadn't mentioned him in his reply email since she'd discreetly asked about him. Maybe she was making more of it than she should be, but it was too much of a coincidence, wasn't it? And the fact that he'd shown up to help her now had her asking even more questions than before. Had Adam sent him to watch over her? No, that made no sense either. She'd barely seen Gabe around, something a good tail would be able to accomplish, but that would also mean she'd never have been able to follow him like she had. Besides, why would Adam have her followed? He wasn't *that* paranoid.

Releasing a sigh, she pulled the door open and stepped out into the hall with determined steps. It was time for the gala and she and Addie's creations to be announced. She wouldn't let thoughts of conspiracies or investigations cloud her excitement for the night.

The dinner was fabulous and she found her tablemates to be intriguing. Sadly, Addie was nowhere to be found, but just as the time was arriving for the award to be announced and the desserts introduced, she spotted her friend on the other side of the room. Making her excuses, she slipped around the dining room and dance floor and joined Addie.

"There you are. I was starting to think *I* was going to have to take all the credit tonight."

Addie gave a halfhearted laugh but it did nothing to change to pale look on her face. She shot a glance over her shoulder nervously. "Are you all right?" Margot asked.

"F-Fine. Yes, I'm—I'm fine."

Margot wasn't convinced but the lights dimmed and a spotlight highlighted the table in the middle of the room. It illuminated a masterful display of pastries to tantalize the guests.

"Where's Noah?" Margot asked. "Isn't he supposed to be here to accept the award as well?"

"I-I don't know." Addie answered one question but was too distracted to register both questions, her gaze unfocused in front of her.

Margot fought the urge to place her hands on either side of the woman and give her a firm shake to bring her out of the daze, but she was afraid it would do no good. Besides, now wasn't the time or the place.

They were called up on stage and she stood next to Addie, impressed at her friend's forced smile. It was fake, but it would be hard to tell from the audience. It was obviously something she'd perfected in many competitions before.

The lights were bright and the announcer, one of the performers who took on the role of MC, began to highlight Addie's many accomplishments and the various awards the ship had been given because of her expertise.

Margot found her attention wandering around the room. She tried to look interested in what the man was saying about her troubled friend, but then her gaze caught on Noah. He was slowly, almost sneakily, making his way around the back of the room. Was he trying to avoid being seen so they wouldn't bring him up on stage? He was as much a part of this as Addie, and certainly more so than Margot.

Then, as she glanced back to where she'd seen him last, he stopped behind one of the furthest tables. He stood against the wall and looked to be waiting for something. But what? Then, as Margot watched, keeping her gaze moving over the room but always coming back to Noah's location, she watched in astonishment as Brice walked past and unobtrusively passed something to Noah, pausing for the briefest of words before he continued on. She thought she caught Noah's imperceptible nod.

She jerked her gaze away, hoping they hadn't noticed her watching them, but when her eyes landed on another area of the room, this time she actually gasped, though thankfully it was quiet.

There, in the back of the room wearing a tuxedo and looking like he belonged in a James Bond movie—or the gala night—stood Detective Adam Eastwood.

~

"WHAT IN THE *world* are you doing here?" Margot demanded.

"I'm not sure if you're pleased to see me or…angry? And can I just say that dress…" He shook his head, expelling a breath. "It's better than the red one."

She grinned, knowing he'd think as much, but soon the grin faded. "Seriously, Adam, why are you here?" She didn't know why, but her heart was pounding. She was sure it had something to do with the ramifications of all of this, but at least a small part of the palpitations was due to how handsome he looked in a tux.

Something she didn't need to notice right now. She couldn't afford to be distracted. If Adam was here, something was going on. She had a gut feeling and those were almost never wrong.

"It's a long story."

She placed her hands on her hips and he took it as an invitation to admire the dress again.

"Really, Margie, that dress…" He shook his head.

"You're doing it again. Getting tongue-tied over a dress. It's *just* a dress."

His grin widened. "You're right. It *is* just a dress, but you make it look amazing."

Now Margot blushed, unable to let his comments slide off. She liked the fact that he thought her beautiful and wasn't ashamed to say it. It did a woman well to be complimented. Yet, his timing could have been better.

"About what I said in my email—" she began.

"Will you dance with me?" he asked, his eyes locked on hers.

She let out a sigh. "You're not going to give this up, are you?"

"Nope. Not until you agree to one dance. Just one?" He looked at her with sparkling hazel eyes and a boyish grin she'd found she had trouble resisting.

"All right," she gave in, accepting his proffered hand.

In her mind, a dance just meant she could explain the situation to him in close proximity, which would better ensure no one overheard them.

They slipped into an easy rhythm and she let them sink into the dance first, finding that she enjoyed being in Adam's arms more than she should. Then again, it *had* been five years since she'd lost her husband. It didn't mean she'd lost her love for him—she wasn't sure she'd ever stop loving him and she'd come to terms with that—but she had gained an appreciation for the fact that her heart could feel again. She certainly felt things toward Adam, though at the moment they were overshadowed by her curiosity as to why he was here and the reality that something was going on—she just didn't know what.

"There was a murder—" she began.

"Oh, Margie," he said in a disappointed tone, "are you really going to ruin our dance with talk of murder? And wasn't it ruled drug overdose? Not murder?"

She gaped at him. "How did you know that?"

"Just call me…informed.'"

"What are you up to, Adam Eastwood?" she asked, her eyes narrowing.

"I may or may not have done some digging before coming out here."

"What type of digging? And why *are* you out here?"

"Is saying I missed you too cheesy?"

She rolled her eyes. "What's the real reason?"

He was about to answer when a commotion at the back of the dining room drew their attention. A young purser came rushing into the room, tears streaming down her face. She rushed blindly forward, making her way toward the captain. A few crewmembers moved to intercept her but she shook them off, only stopping in front of the stoic man.

They watched as the woman explained something with frantic hand motions and then burst into tears. As her news was conveyed, the captain shot to his feet, a look of concern washing over his handsome features. Then he motioned to two men who Margot knew were part of the security team, and they left the room. The third security team member ushered the sobbing woman out after them as well.

"I don't know about you, but I don't think people are supposed to cry like that on cruises."

She glanced up to see a look of genuine concern on Adam's face despite his sarcastic tone. He wasn't one to make light of troublesome situations, though his humor in all areas of life was one of the things Margot appreciated most about the detective. She could see on his hardened features that his detective sense was kicking in. "What do you say we go see what's up?"

Margot was stunned at his suggestion but leapt at the chance. "I thought you'd never ask."

They made their way off of the dance floor and then, as discretely as possible, slipped out of the same door the captain and the men had. Adam slipped his hand around hers and she felt the warmth sink past their hands to her heart. She'd missed him.

The hallway they had stepped into extended in both ways but they heard hushed voices coming from the right. Looking at one another, they set off toward the voices. The hall curved and they pulled up before coming into view of an open door ahead. A sign above it indicated

"Security Office." Margot's stomach clenched—this didn't look good.

"This was not an accident."

At the words, Adam's hand squeezed Margot's.

"This was clearly thought out. Murder."

"But he's not—"

Adam released her hand and stepped forward. "I heard murder. Can I help?"

Margot suppressed a smile at Adam's direct approach, but followed him to the entrance of the office.

"And who are you?" Margot recognized Harvey Pearson, the ship security officer.

"I'm Detective Adam Eastwood." Adam took out his credentials and showed them to the man.

Harvey's brow furrowed. "Detective? From *Virginia*?"

"And liaison to the FBI," a voice said behind them.

Margot and Adam both turned around.

"Gabe?" Margot exclaimed.

"We meet again," he said, smiling at Margot. "You just seem to be everywhere, don't you, Mrs. Durand?"

Margot noticed Adam's intent look at her but thankfully Gabe continued.

"I'm Gabe Williams with the FBI," he said, flashing an official badge at Harvey. "I've asked Adam to join me here."

Now Margot shot Adam a look that demanded an explanation, but she knew now wasn't the time or the place.

"What is going on?" Gabe asked.

"I—" Harvey began.

Just then they all heard footsteps pounding down the hall and they turned to see the captain with the crying woman at his side, another security guard as his escort.

"Captain," Harvey said, standing straighter.

"What is going on here?" the captain demanded.

"Gabe Williams with the FBI."

"And…" The captain's eyebrows rose and his gaze moved to Adam and then Margot, frowning.

"Detective Adam Eastwood and Mrs. Margot—"

"Durand. Yes, I know of Mrs. Durand, but I don't know *why* she's here."

"Mrs. Durand and I are…acquainted," Adam said with a forced smile.

"Yes, but I don't think having a *guest* here during this, um, time is appropriate."

"And can you tell me exactly what's going on here, Captain?" Gabe said, ignoring the Captain's hesitance about Margot.

"At the moment, I—"

A young crewmember wearing a medical coat ran down the hall toward them, his gaze solely focused on the captain. "Sir, he's dead."

Margot felt the stab of the words, her stomach clenching at the reality that another death had occurred on board the *Carrousel Luxury*.

"Who is?" Gabe said, stepping forward.

The young man looked to the captain and then back to Gabe. At an almost imperceptible nod from the captain, the young man cleared his throat. "Michael Bowers."

# CHAPTER 9

MARGOT SAT on the deck attached to her cabin looking out over the lights of Ensenada. They would depart later that night and begin their travel back, but her mind was overloaded with the events of the evening. First, finding out that there had been another death, then discovering it had been the somewhat stiff but organized Michael Bowers, it was almost too much to take in. What was going on?

Margot had faded into the background as details were demanded and credentials shared, but soon the captain put his foot down and demanded—albeit politely—that Margot go back to her cabin as they dealt with the details of the death. Begrudgingly, she'd purchased a coffee and made her way back to her room, waiting for Adam to come knocking on the door. That had been hours ago.

The sound of a light tap made her jolt forward, the wrap

draped over her knees slipping, and she rushed to answer it.

"Adam," she said, relief flowed by concern rushed through her. He looked exhausted with dark circles under his eyes and his shoulders slumped, but he offered her a soft smile.

"May I come in for a bit?"

"Of course," she said, ushering him into the small space. "Do you want me to order you something?"

"No, I grabbed a bite to eat with Gabe before coming to see you."

"The balcony is nice," she offered.

He smiled and nodded, following her out. They sat in the chairs that angled toward one another and she resisted the urge to demand what he'd discovered. For a few minutes, he just stared out at the city, the lights blinking and the faint sounds of music coming from somewhere, probably one of the many restaurants still open to tourists. The breeze was warm, though by no means hot, and the scent of salt hung in the air.

Finally, he shifted and leaned forward, elbows on his knees. "I probably shouldn't do this, but I'm going to fill you in."

Margot felt the sense of apprehension fill her. What was going on? What would Adam tell her about what had happened? Would they know what was behind it?

"You don't have to," she began, knowing she desperately wanted to know what was going on but that she didn't want to put Adam in a bad position for sharing things with her.

"I asked Gabe, told him of our history, and he agreed. He also hinted that you may already know more than you should." She heard the humor in Adam's voice and part of her relaxed.

"So, as you heard, Michael Bowers died. The woman we saw rush into the room tonight was a friend of Bowers and had just been informed from local authorities that he'd been the victim of a brutal stabbing in Ensenada. They rushed him on board and the woman came to notify the captain, but...as you saw, it was too late."

Margot's mind jumped to several things at once. Stabbing. That meant murder. But when had it happened? Where?

"What time was he stabbed? Where?" Adam's eyebrows rose and she felt ashamed. "I'm sorry. It's awful that he's dead, terrible, but I'm wondering..." She didn't finish her sentence because she wasn't sure that she could. She didn't have all of the necessary information yet, but there were several things that weren't adding up. Like Noah. She pictured him at the back of the gala tonight. What had he given Brice?

"WE'RE NOT SURE. His body will need to be examined by a

M.E. The best the doc could say was it was recent, and not too far from the ship."

This caused Margot to frown. "But all of the less friendly neighborhoods are further away from port."

"I know." Adam leveled his gaze on her.

Had Brice paid off Noah for killing Michael? But no, there was no way he would have had time to do it. It was pure conjecture and there was no evidence…then again, she *had* followed Brice to that restaurant and it did sound as if things were going on. But Noah? What part did he play in all of this? If any at all.

"Before you go piecing things together, wait until you hear this."

"Are you finally going to tell me why you're here on my cruise ship?"

"*Your* ship, huh?"

"You know what I mean," she said with a smile.

"Well, like Gabe said, he asked me to come. Or…maybe what's more accurate is that I demanded for him to get me on board. Among some other strings I pulled, I was able to get down here quickly."

"But why? What about your assignment? Your lecturing?"

He shrugged. "Why? Because of your overly innocent little email digging for clues. I know you better than you think, Margot Durand." He offered a tired smile. "I wasn't about to let you have a mysterious adventure without me. Besides, I wanted to make sure you were safe."

Warmth surged through her at his words and she felt a light blush color her cheeks, thankfully hidden by the darkness. "Thank you, but I wasn't sure, until now, that it *was* something mysterious. Clearly, we have a murderer on our hands."

"We?"

"I suppose it's you and Gabe then. Did you know that Gabe was FBI?"

"About that..." He shifted back in his seat and she saw him shake his head. "Turns out Gabe has been running an undercover operation dealing with some pretty interesting things. Even the woman who was murdered—"

"So it *was* murder?"

"Definitely— Well, we can't say for sure until the M.E. confirms, but Gabe assures me she never would have taken drugs. She was an undercover agent."

Margot gasped. "She was?"

"Yes, she's been working with none other than Michael Bowers. Apparently, he's involved in some pretty terrifying things, including but not limited to drug and gem smuggling from Ensenada."

"Really," she said, leaning back in her chair and trying to

piece it all together. She hadn't interacted with Michael much, but he hadn't looked like a smuggler. Then again, what did a smuggler really look like?

"Yes. Kristen had been working closely with him but there was another piece to all of this: a contact who works on the ship but didn't reveal his—or her—identity. They would leave notes in certain locations for Kristen and Michael. It's the only reason she was staying undercover, she wanted to nail all of the components in this ring. She'd been working on the local side of things until this silent partner got her a job on board the ship recently."

"But then she was murdered. Was she suspected then? Is that why she died?"

"That's unclear at this point."

"I can't believe it." Margot leaned forward, her elbows on her knees. She'd known something was going on, but she never would have imagined smuggling.

"That's the thing, there are more things involved than just a simple smuggling operation—if there even is such a thing."

"What about Brice?"

Adam hesitated a moment. "Brice? Brice who?"

"Brice Simmons."

"The actor?"

"Yes." Margot stared at him, surprised he didn't know what she was talking about. "What's his part in all of this?"

"I, uh... Gabe didn't say."

Margot's heart pounded. They didn't know of Brice's involvement? Surely he was involved in *some* way. There were too many things going on to not have him as part of the operation, now that she knew there was an operation. Then again, was he involved or had she merely seen a man hand something to a crewmember? But that seemed like too much of a coincidence, especially after what she'd overheard at the restaurant that day.

She filled Adam in on what she'd done that afternoon and what she knew of Brice.

"Sounds like he's definitely mixed up in this then—at least in part. I'll need to discuss it with Gabe. But you..." He shook his head. "You know better than to go off on your own like that, Margie." He looked worried but she assured him she'd been fine.

"But still—" he began.

Then another thought occurred to her and she interrupted his next lecture fueled by worry. "Addie isn't mixed up in this, is she?"

"Your friend, the pastry chef?"

"Yes," Margot said, nervously twisting her hands together. "She's been acting so strange and, I don't know, almost looking guilty."

"Gabe didn't mention her, but he didn't mention Brice either. All he said is that he's certain that there is at least one more member of this team to consider—and there could be more."

The reality sunk into Margot's chest and she felt despair take root. Addie acted guilty. She had been moody, gone often, and distracted. Was it possible? Were those signs of guilt or was she hiding something condemning like being involved in a smuggling ring?

Margot didn't want to believe it, but she knew that the only way to clear it all up was to have a conversation. Something she would do the very next morning.

THE NEXT MORNING, Margot woke to bright sunlight streaming through the thin curtains she'd pulled closed the night before as Adam left. He'd promised that they could trace down leads in the morning after breakfast with Gabe, but her mind had been set on seeing Addie. She didn't want to believe that her friend could be involved with something like a smuggling ring, but there had to be some explanation for her evasive behavior. But what could be so important that Addie wouldn't have shared with Margot?

She pulled the drapes aside and saw nothing but ocean stretching out before her. It was a stunning sight, the water registering a deep, azure blue. She could stare at this view for hours, but the press of the case was too persistent. She showered, dressed, and was out the door early.

Cringing, she knocked on Adam's door.

After a few shuffling footsteps, he opened the door wearing a bright blue polo with khaki shorts and a sleepy grin. His hair was adorably mussed and she resisted the urge to reach up and smooth it down. They needed to focus on the case, not the fact that she wanted him to remind her of the sweetness of his kiss.

"Ready?" she said, hands on hips.

He just shook his head. "Give me a moment to at least run a comb through my hair."

Grinning, she followed him into his room and looked around. Clothes were strewn everywhere and the top of his small desk was covered in papers.

"Didn't you just get here last night?"

"Yeah," he said distractedly from the bathroom.

"Then how is it possible you made this big of a mess?"

He didn't answer right away but, when he came out of the bathroom with slicked down hair and a big grin, he shrugged innocently. "I'm usually tidy, but there's something about being away on a trip—vacation or not—that makes me feel like I don't need to constrain myself to tidiness norms."

"You goof," she said, smiling.

"So, to breakfast?"

"Yes."

His grin widened and she led him down their hall and out the door into the early morning air. It was cooler, the breeze from the ocean coming in stiff gusts, but soon they were back inside and heading to a buffet.

Gabe met them at the entrance and led them to a table in the back. Once they had their food, they ate in silence for a few moments before he jumped in.

"What can you tell me, Margot?"

Her eyebrows rose. "And what makes you think I know anything?" Her coy response made Adam smile and Gabe shook his head.

"Look, I saw you around the ship the first day. I was going to say something, but it could have compromised my situation. I'm registered here under the name Josh Wilkes and I couldn't have you coming up and saying you knew me as Gabe."

"I understand," she said, nodding. "But I have one question."

"Shoot," he said, taking a bite of light green honeydew.

"Why were you near the sports storage area where Kristen was found?"

He grinned, chewing and then swallowing before he could answer her. "So it was you following me."

She inclined her head.

"You're quicker than I anticipated. Nice catch," he said to Adam with a wink. "I was looking for Kirsten. We were supposed to meet that night. I'd seen her in the club, acting like we didn't know each other. She said she'd been called to a face-to-face meeting with her contact. It was supposed to be our big break. We'd arranged to meet at the storage area.

"I'd just gotten there and slipped inside, hoping to avoid whoever—well, now I know it was you—but then I got a text from her saying that the meeting had been canceled so I left and the passage was clear on my way back."

"I hid in a laundry closet," she said with a shrug.

"Clever."

"She couldn't have sent that text though, could she?"

He pressed his lips together. "We believe her contact found out about who she really was. I think they were the one to message me, likely thinking they were buying themselves time before Kristen was discovered."

"But then I heard something—or someone—else in there after you'd walked past, which drew my attention."

"And you found her," Gabe said, his expression pained.

"Yes. Do you think that whoever killed her left out the back door? No one passed by me after you left."

"It's possible." Gabe broke a piece of bacon in half. "Or they were already gone."

"I've got a question," Margot said, her forehead wrinkling. "Do you have *any* idea who her contact could be? I mean, there have to be some suspects."

"There are a few people I've been keeping an eye on, but whoever it is is very careful and covers their tracks well."

"You should tell him what you saw," Adam said, finally speaking up after spending considerable amount of time working through his eggs and toast.

"What do you mean? What did you see?" Gabe leaned forward, elbows on the table cradling a cup of hot coffee in his hands.

She explained seeing Brice pass something to Noah as well as the conversation she'd overheard between Brice and his assistants and how she'd followed him to see what was going on. She recapped the conversation he'd had with Gold Chain but also how the trail had run cold when Gabe had rescued her.

"Why were you there, though?" she asked Gabe. "If you didn't suspect Brice, why were you following Andres?"

"We *don't* suspect Brice…at least not yet, but I have had my suspicions about José Luis Martinez—the one you call Gold Chain," he said with a grin. "He owns that restaurant you were at and many other businesses catering to tourists. He's done well for himself, no doubt, but we think he's done a little *too* well for the operations he has going. I've been down to Ensenada quite a bit recently and I'm usually staked out by whatever restaurant he's in. I saw you sneaking around and, when you came out to follow Andres as well, I knew something was up. I had no idea you were following Brice, though."

"So you think the restaurant is a front then?" Margot asked. Her mind started to piece things together.

"We can't definitively say, nor does it affect us. What's really our problem is anything that goes on on board the ships that come into port and anything affecting U.S. Citizens." Gabe looked over to Adam. "You know how it is. We've got leads everywhere but nothing solid. Though we have some cooperation with the officials in Ensenada, we need proof. Martinez has covered his tracks well and whatever happens on U.S. soil is covered up just as quickly."

Adam nodded, his lips pressed into a hard line as he thought through the situation.

"What if Brice *is* involved though?"

"We'd need evidence. Besides—what do you think? He hired *Noah* to kill his own partner? It doesn't add up. Noah isn't even on our radar."

Margot thought this through. *Should* Noah be on their radar? She thought of him coming in late and his lie about where he'd been. People lied all the time though, and for various reasons. Then again, the reality of two murders was enough to bring anyone into question.

"If he is involved and he's working with Noah, it's possible Kristen was found out. Or perhaps..." She paused. "Then there's Michael Bowers. You say he's a part of this...so is it possible whoever is behind this is eliminating partners for a reason?"

"It's possible," Gabe said, steepling his fingers. "Kristen said she hardly interacted with Bowers. They worked independently of each other though they did know about one another. She made it clear their instructions were that they weren't to be seen together—at all." Gabe sighed, leaning back in his chair. "I'm so frustrated. I've been working this case for over a year now. The drugs are coming into the U.S. and we've all but pinpointed the *Carousel* cruise line, not just this ship but several of them, but there is never any concrete evidence. And why drugs *and* jewels?"

Margot didn't have an answer for this but something Gabe said made her think of another angle. Addie. She had signed on to the *Carousel* cruise line a little under a year ago.

Something wasn't right there and she had to find out what exactly was the problem.

"Sorry." Gabe tossed his napkin onto the empty plate before him. "I need to go. I've got a ship to shore call set up and it's imperative I make that. I'm afraid it'll be hard for me to get straight answers around here now that my cover is blown. I'd appreciate it if you keep your eyes and ears open to anything."

"Of course," Adam said, shaking his friend's hand.

"Margot," Gabe said then strode away.

She watched him go, wondering what was next. Someone had killed Kristen and now Michael. They had no suspects and no tangible leads. How was that possible?

"I know that look," Adam said. "Where to first, Watson?"

She smiled, standing up and tossing her napkin down. "We're going to see a woman about a pastry. And it's Holmes," she added with a wink.

# CHAPTER 10

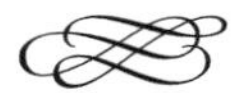

THE MIDMORNING CROWD was in full swing, those who had slept in late making their way to the buffets and restaurants for breakfast. Margot wasn't interested in anyone else at this moment. She only had one person on her list to visit. She had a feeling that, once she was able to clear her friend and find out the truth, she would truly be able to focus on the case at hand and, with Adam by her side, help solve the murderous mystery.

They turned down the hall that led to the crew quarters and Margot stopped in front of Addie's door. She let out a breath and turned to look at Adam. He smiled at her and she felt her spirits renewed. It was nice to have someone with her.

She raised her hand to knock but the door swung inward. Curiosity and worry got the best of Margot and she pushed it further in, stopping only when she got a clear view into the room.

"Addie?" she gasped.

In front of her, embracing a man whose back was to them, Addie was locked in a passionate kiss.

At the sound of Margot's surprised exclamation, Addie jerked back from the man, stepping a full two feet back and covering her lips with her hand. Her flush made her look sixteen years old instead of thirty-two.

"M-Margot?" she stammered.

When Margot finally pulled her gaze from her friend to that of the man, she gasped again. "Captain?"

He stammered something but fell silent, his gaze jerking to Addie then dropping to the floor. Margot thought of the first day when she'd overheard the crewmembers talking about the captain having an affair. Was it with her friend?

"I'm new here, but I've got a feeling you don't kiss all of your crewmembers like that," Adam said, gently pushing Margot into the room and closing the door behind them for privacy. She was almost too shocked to register what was happening, but then she realized that Adam was being discrete for her friend's sake.

"Oh my," Addie finally said, shaking her head. "This is it. I can't take it anymore, Grayson. I just can't."

He gave her a pained look but then his features softened and he smiled at her, reaching out to take her hand. "Let me." He turned to look at them. "Margot, Detective Eastwood, we're engaged to be married."

It took a few moments for the words to sink in to understanding. "You're not married?"

It was the captain's turn to look surprised, then realization dawned and he sighed. "There are those on board who like to make up stories. I am not, nor have I ever been, married. I *do* like to keep my private life just that—private. I'm afraid that leaves too much room for minds to wander and imagine."

Margot burst into a wide grin. "That's fantastic!" Then she laughed. "I mean, that you're engaged."

Now Addie beamed, looking back up at the handsome man beside her. He was several years older than she, but Margot could see instantly the love they shared. "I'm so happy Marg."

"I suppose we owe you an apology. Or, rather, *I* do." The captain shook his head. "I've been captain of this ship for two years now and I've never looked at any of my crewmembers with anything more than leadership in mind...until I met Addie." He sighed and took another moment to study her face before looking back at them. "But, in my position of leadership, it's a tenuous thing for the captain to be in a relationship—of any kind—with a crewmember. It's not against company policy, just so we're clear, but it can affect how the crew perceives me as well as Addie."

Margot was beginning to guess what had happened. "You're hiding the engagement."

Addie nodded. "I would have told you, Marg. I wanted to and it's caused no end to arguments between us. I understand Grayson is trying to protect me, but you are one of my closest friends... It's just that I couldn't risk someone like Noah overhearing. It's been murder on me to keep it from you."

Margot felt the relief of her friend's confession at the same time she felt the reminder of how serious their true mission was on this ship—not to uncover secret engagements, but to catch a killer.

"Then I wish you both happiness and can assure you that neither I nor Adam will share your secret—right?" She grinned up at Adam, who nodded.

"Did you need something?" Addie said, shyly looking back at the captain.

"No," Margot said smiling as she walked to the door, pulling on Adam's arm. "I'm so happy for you both."

"That was a dead end," Adam said once they were in the hallway. "Though I can't say they aren't inspiring."

Margot's stomach clenched at his words. Did he mean their engagement? But no, she couldn't allow herself to think about that—not now. Besides, that couldn't have been what Adam was talking about...could it?

Pushing the thoughts from her mind, she tugged on Adam's sleeve. "Come on. I've got an idea."

~

THEY SEARCHED through Kristen's room after getting permission from Gabe. Clothes of all colors and styles cluttered the small cabinet that was hers in the four-person room. All the other crewmembers were on duty, which gave them a window of privacy.

"I've got nothing," Adam said, standing up and stretching as best he could in the cramped space. "You?"

"Nothing." Margot dropped the sequined pink miniskirt that matched the one Kristen had been wearing when Margot found her. Sighing, she ran a hand over her hair. She'd been sure there would have been something for them to find, anything that could tie Brice to the whole thing, but there was nothing.

She stepped toward the door but stopped, looking back over the area. If she were Kristen and she was working undercover, where would she hide something she didn't want any of her roommates to find—either accidentally or on purpose? The logical place would be under the mattress, but most people would check there first so Margot hadn't been surprised when it was empty.

Adam stood from where he'd been examining the empty space below the drawers under her bottom bunk when he hit his head.

"Ouch!" he cried out, his hand reaching up to rub a spot on the top of his head.

"Careful, you're not exactly made for this space." She smiled but then froze. He wasn't made for this space. No tall person was.

"What?" Adam said, recognizing the look on her face. "You've got an idea."

She stepped to the tall dresser to the end of the ladies' beds. One side held one girl's clothes and the other held Kristen's. She looked down at the bottom and noticed the woman's shoes.

"She was tall, wasn't she," Margot said to herself, holding up a size ten shoe. "Taller than her crewmates." She looked through the other women's compartments, careful not to disturb anything. "Adam, look on the top of the closet! Is there anything up there?"

Adam reached up, his nose wrinkling at the effort. He was tall, but Kristen would have been even taller in her four-inch heels. Then his eyes shot open. "I've got something."

Margot waited patiently as he pulled out a handkerchief and stretched to reach whatever it was. Finally, with a grunt, he pulled down a stack of written notes. Excitement bubbled up in her.

"What are they?" she asked as Adam riffled through.

"Looks like they are written in some sort of code. Probably nothing too complicated. I think…" His voice trailed off as he read through a few, careful not to touch any of them. "I think they are pick up and drop off locations. Though it's difficult to tie these to Kristen exactly. I'm assuming they're hers, but..."

Margot leaned forward. "May I see one?"

He angled one toward her, holding it open with the handkerchief, and she gasped. "I know that writing."

"You do?" He was shocked.

Margot stepped back, blinking. "It's Noah's. Noah Spence."

"The guy who bakes? The *same* guy who you saw talking with Brice?"

"Yes!" She frantically ran through all that she knew about Noah. He had seemed upset about Kristen's death, but was it sadness or anger? Had he been the one to kill her? And what of Michael Bowers? Had he also been involved with that? And what about Brice? How was he involved with any of this?

"Talk to me, Margie," Adam said, his gaze intent on her. "Tell me what's going on in that brain of yours."

She blinked rapidly. It was all starting to come together, but in order to crack the case, they would need the involvement of the FBI and a few well-placed visits in Ensenada. "Is the FBI really working with the authorities in Ensenada?"

Adam frowned. “If Gabe says so, then yes, he'll be in contact with local authorities.”

“Then I need to talk with him. And I need to talk with someone else too.”

Adams eyebrows rose. “Are you going to fill me in?”

She smiled up at him, brushing off a swatch of dust from his shoulder. “Always.”

# CHAPTER 11

MARGOT CLUTCHED her canvas bag with one hand, the strap slung over her shoulder, and her floppy hat with the other as she made her way across the crowded deck to the more private deck at the back of the ship. The moment she turned the corner, the wind died down somewhat due to the partition, and she let go of her hat.

There, reclining in a blue-cushioned chaise lounge, lay Brice Simmons. His chest bare and tanned, shining with a recent application of some type of tanning oil, no doubt applied by one of the bikini-clad women on either side of him.

Margot fought the urge to roll her eyes as she approached, hoping she got what she wanted out of this meeting.

"Hello, Brice," she said with a bright smile.

Brice moved, his hand reaching up to push the dark and expensive sunglasses onto the top of his head. He looked surprised to see her, but in a pleasant way.

"Margot. It's good to see you. Will you sit?"

He looked to the side where one of his assistants was already getting up.

"Actually, I was wondering if we could talk…just you and I?"

His surprise grew, but so did his smile. "Absolutely. Ladies, will you give us a few minutes?"

The former police officer, Haden, looked ready to argue with him but then she looked at Margot. Likely assuming Margot was no threat to her boss, she followed the other woman down the deck.

Brice smiled again, patting the lounge next to him. "Please."

She sat, leaving her legs on the ground and propping her elbows on her knees to look at him. "What I have to say may not be pleasant," she began.

He replaced his sunglasses and his eyebrows hiked, but he didn't say anything, allowing her the room to explain.

"You see, I followed you into Ensenada. I saw where you went."

He tried hard not to let his emotions show but she caught a glimpse, the quickest flutter of movement, in response to her words.

“I heard what José Luis Martinez said to you. I also know that you know Kristen Chambers’s death wasn’t an accident. It was murder.”

Brice sat up, more like jerked up, and yanked off his sunglasses. “You don’t know anything.” His gaze drilled into Margot but she didn't flinch.

“But I do, Brice. I think you are working with people on this ship to smuggle drugs into America.”

“Drugs? No. Absolutely not. We do *not* smuggle drugs,” he said, the color in his tanned cheeks flushing red. “I would never—” He ground his teeth and looked out to the ocean. “I would never do that. Not after my sister.”

She remembered his story about his sister. So he had been telling the truth. That meant it was time for Margot to take the next step.

“Look, the FBI is on this case. They are going to finger you in the smuggling. It’s no use for you to deny it. They’ll find the drugs.”

“There are no drugs!”

“Don’t deny it,” Margot pushed. “I know you met with José and the FBI are already looking into his business. They’ll find your drug connection and that’ll be it.”

"I'm telling you, Margot," he said, leaning toward her with fury in his gaze. "No drugs."

"Then what aren't you telling me, Brice? Because the police are going to find all the evidence they need. There was an undercover agent. It's over. And, from where I sit, your sister would be disgusted with you." It was a low blow, one she was loath to make, but she had to push him to a certain point

"I would never do that! Not drugs. Never. Not for anyone." His features fell and he looked out to sea again. "It's gems."

Margot leaned forward, her gaze flicking over Brice's tanned shoulder. "What do you mean?"

"I smuggle gems into the U.S. without paying import taxes."

"Gems?" She had suspected this, but she wanted to be certain. "You met José when you were here filming *Green Flames Rising*, didn't you?" She needed to dig further, to get him to open up more.

"You know a lot for not knowing the truth," he shot back. "Yeah. I met José when he catered some of our meals. He said he had a way for me to make some extra money on the side. It was during that time in my career when my gambling debts were plastered all over magazine covers. He said he could help. That he knew a guy. I was certain I could get them to the right people and sell them for a lot more than they could here in Mexico. There's a hot market in underground Hollywood circles." He sighed, rubbing a hand over his face.

"But not drugs, Margot. Never drugs. I wouldn't..." He broke off and she saw the pain on his features. "I know what they do to people, to families. I'd never be a part of that."

She watched him, looking for any signs of deception, but while he kept his gaze on the ocean in front of him, he gave no indication that he was lying. Lost in painful memories, yes, but not lying.

She nodded slightly and Adam, Gabe, and two of the ship's security officers stepped out from behind the wind partition where they'd been listening to the conversation.

"Mr. Simmons, you're under arrest."

He looked from the men to Margot. "You're with them? What? This whole time?"

"No. Not at first." She shook her head, unsure why she felt the need to explain herself to this arrogant man.

"It's a shame, you know," he said with a rueful grin. "You and I could have made a pretty great power couple. Besides, I love good French pastries. Then again, who knows? I've got access to some great lawyers and I'm sure you'll find that my hands are clean. Friends in high places and all." He winked at her.

She felt the urge to slap him. As if sensing this, Adam

stepped beside her and wrapped a protective arm around her shoulders.

"Good thing I've got friends in high places too."

His hands now cuffed behind him, Brice turned his attention to Adam, his eyes dancing between the man and his arm around Margot.

"Ah, I see. You prefer the more law-abiding type. Well, to each their own."

"Come on, Simmons," Gabe said, rolling his eyes. "Let's go."

Margot watched him go with a mix of sadness and justification. She was glad he had been caught, but now they had to wrap the more pressing—if not more important—angle of how drugs were getting into the U.S. when they weren't tied up in Brice Simmons's operation.

Or were they?

Margot leaned into Adam, letting out a sigh as her mind raced through details. If Brice wasn't involved with drugs, it was a stretch to think he was involved with the murders. She wouldn't rule it out, but she couldn't bring herself to see him complicit in something so sinister. At least the smuggling of gems was purely from a monetary motivational standpoint. But murder? That fell more in line with the drugs, at least in Margot's mind.

"What's on that beautiful mind of yours now?" Adam said, smiling.

"I was just thinking that—if Brice wasn't involved with drugs, what if his contact was involved with them *and* the gems."

"I think I know what you're getting at, but do we have enough proof to arrest him?"

Margot's eyes narrowed as her gaze flew to the water in front of them. "Maybe not yet, but I have a feeling I know how to catch him because I think I know where the gems *and* the drugs are. But it'll require a little bit of planning. Are you up for that?"

"Absolutely."

"Good, because it's crucial we don't make a mistake. I have a feeling this was their last cruise."

"I'M SO sorry about all of this," Addie said as she and Margot sat on the private deck attached to Margot's room. "If I'd had any idea..."

Margot laughed. "You can't guess when murder is going to happen. It's in no way your fault."

"What's next then?" Addie's brown eyes peered at Margot over her steaming cup of coffee.

As much as Margot trusted her friend and wanted to share what was going to happen next, she knew that the less people that knew, the better.

"I'm afraid I can't say, but I wanted to take a few minutes before we docked to chat with you and make sure everything was all right. We've barely seen each other on this cruise—for good reason—but first and foremost, you're my friend and I care about you and what's happening in your life. I know you couldn't open up to me before, but if there's anything you wanted to share now, I wanted to let you know that I'm here for you. I was once your age and in love—" Margot smirked at how old saying that made her feel. "—and I relied heavily on my friends during that time."

Addie sighed and turned her gaze out to the ocean. Land was just visible in the distance and, with their arrival, plans would be set in motion that would end everything. At least Margot hoped so.

"It's just frustrating," Addie said, looking back at Margot finally. "I love Grayson so much and I know he's the right guy. Like, he asked me to marry him and I had no doubts, but sometimes he's just...so frustrating."

Margot chuckled. "I understand. Men look at things very different."

"Very."

"But you guys are talking about it, right? That's the important part. To keep communication lines open."

"Oh yes." Addie nodded emphatically. "We talked a lot after you and Adam left. I think it was good. After this nightmare of a cruise is over, things should settle down. Again, I'm so sorry."

"Really, it's okay."

They both looked off into the distance until Addie spoke up again. "So, Adam…"

Margot smiled, knowing what her friend was getting at. "He's a good friend."

"More than a friend?"

"Maybe."

"Sure," Addie laughed. "I saw the way he looks at you, though. He definitely cares for you. How do you feel about that? After Julian and all."

Margot let her friend's question sink in. How did she feel? Then again, it was hard to pinpoint her own feelings when, in the back of her mind, she was still cycling through the logistics she'd worked out with Gabe and Adam. But, didn't that count for something? The very reality of her reliance on Adam and her trust in him spoke volumes.

"He's a good man. Similar to Julian in some ways but very different in others. I…" Margot felt the faint flush and chided herself for reacting so childishly about it all. "I really care for him."

"Good." Addie reached across and gripped her hand. "You deserve happiness. Especially after…" Her words trailed off but Margot didn't need her to say any more. Julian's death had been unexpected and mysterious, a shock to Margot as well as anyone who had known her husband. Then again, his job had been dangerous and she'd known that. But still...

"Margot?"

Drawn from her thoughts, Margot looked up and met her friend's gaze. "Thanks again for coming. It was only fitting that I received this award with the person who helped me become what I am today."

"You had a lot of amazing teachers."

Addie shrugged. "But you were the one who taught me to love being a baker, not merely the art of it." She stood, letting out a sigh. "I'd better get back to the kitchen. Noah will be cleaning up in preparation for disembarking. We've got a week off of this ship while it undergoes some new construction so that means vacation for the crew, but a massive move for certain areas—the kitchen being one."

Margot sat up straighter. "Oh? What does that mean?"

"Nothing too major. We just have to get any extra supplies off when usually we'd let some sit. Our food overflow gets donated to a charity in the area, which Noah oversees, but I want to make sure things are flowing smoothly. They'll officially pull everything off tomorrow, but I have the day off so I'll just check in now."

"I understand," Margot said, following Addie to the door.

"Let's see if we can all do dinner—Grayson included—toward the end of this week then."

"I'd really like that. I'll let you know."

Margot watched her friend walk back down the hall as more pieces fell into place. She had to update Adam and Gabe.

# CHAPTER 12

NIGHT HAD FALLEN across the dock, the sounds of water traffic much decreased at the late hour. There were still workers going back and forth, but they were confined to the warehouse areas instead of near the gangplank that led to the aft entrance for the crewmembers.

Margot walked arm and arm with Brice as they made their way up the gangplank. Her heart pounded in her ears, but she continued to remind herself that they would be safe. No matter what, Adam would watch out for her and she knew that.

"This isn't a good idea." Brice swallowed hard, not even looking at her.

"You're making the right choice, Brice. I think at heart you're a good guy, but you've made some poor choices. Think of your sister—she'd want you to do this."

He nodded almost imperceptibly and kept going. "You're right. She would. You kind of remind me of her."

Margot wasn't sure how to take that. His sister had been a drug addict and eventually overdosed.

"I mean, before the drugs," he added quickly. They were almost to the outside door where a dim light shone out from the hall inside. "She was smart, observant, and wouldn't take no for an answer."

Margot smiled despite the situation. "Thanks."

They approached the door and Brice reached out.

"Easy," a voice said into the earpiece she'd concealed under her hair. "You're doing great, Margie."

She resisted the urge to react to Adam's nickname. Instead, they walked inside and Brice led the way toward the kitchen.

"Okay," Adam's voice whispered in her ear, "time to put on the act."

Brice wasn't wearing an earpiece so she whispered to him. "Here comes the act." He nodded and she let out a peal of feminine laughter as they came up on the kitchen door. "Oh Brice, you're too funny."

He pushed the door in and she stepped into the kitchen with him.

There, at the back by the pantry door, Noah stood surrounded by bags of flour. "What in the—" He pulled out a gun, aiming first at Brice then at Margot. "Margot? What is *she* doing here?"

"Noah?" Margot said, trying to sound pleasantly surprised. "You're his contact?"

He frowned, his gaze flying to Brice's. "What is going on? What does she know?" he demanded.

"Dude, chill." Brice patted Margot's hand woven through his arm. "She's with me now."

"I'll repeat myself," Noah said, still leveling the gun at Margot, "What is *she* doing here? Where is Haden?"

"She's my new partner," Brice explained. "And please, man, put the gun down. This is a civilized operation."

It lowered a fraction of an inch. "I don't get it." His gaze rotated to Margot. "What are you doing here?"

"I want in on the action," she said with a smile. "I've gotten to know Brice here on the cruise, and he let me in on the sweet deal you guys have going on down here. I wanted in."

The gun rose again. "Absolutely not."

"Oh come on," Margot said. "I may run a pastry shop, but that's not all I do." She flashed a cunning grin his way.

Noah looked interested for a moment before his mask slid into place again.

"I'm in the import-export business, if you know what I

mean," Margot said, rehearsing what Gabe had told her to say. "I'd be a valuable asset to this organization. I took this opportunity to see if I could do some networking in Ensenada."

"But you're friends with Addie."

"Sure," Margot said, shrugging, "but she hasn't seen me in a while. People change. Desperate times call for desperate measures."

He wasn't buying it, she could tell, but she had to do something to convince him. Then it came to her. She slipped her hand from Brice's arm and stepped forward, trying not to let the gun barrel frighten away her courage. "Look, I know this guy—" She pointed over her shoulder at Brice with her thumb. "—isn't daring. I have a feeling you're the type of guy who sees an opportunity and goes for it. I'm not afraid of getting into...other things. If you know what I mean."

Now Noah looked confused, his gaze going between Margot and Brice. "What is this? Some kind of setup?"

"No," Margot said.

She looked back to Brice, who now looked appropriately angry and she thanked the Lord she was working with an actor.

"Dude, I don't know what she's talking about."

"Drugs," Margot said, putting her hands on her hips. "Plain and simple. I mean we *are* talking about Mexico. If you aren't dealing, you should be, because as nice and clean as gems are, they won't make half the money you could get through dealing. Am I right?" She shot a hardened look at Noah.

She waited, knowing silence was her friend right now. He looked from her to Brice then back to her. He broke into a smile, his gun lowering. "You're kidding. How did you know?"

"What?" Brice exploded from behind Margot. "You're joking, right? You are *not* bringing drugs in. Tell me you aren't, Noah."

She did all she could not to admire Brice's masterful acting job and kept her gaze on the man in front of her.

"You had everything worked out, didn't you, Brice?" Noah said, his laugh cynical. "But you didn't get it. You still don't. So what, your sister overdosed. That's sad, but grow up. Gems do well, but I couldn't live on that. No one could—unless they were some world famous actor." He shook his head.

"What are you talking about?" Brice asked.

"I'm talking about being sick and tired of being your peon. I mean, seriously? Did you think I was going to work for you forever? I started importing drugs almost a year ago and have made double what we made last year."

"Noah—"

"Stop it," Noah yelled, the gun going back up but this time

pointed at Brice. "You have *no* idea what it's like. Day in, day out, saying yes to all these customers demanding things. Working at a job I hate. All of it just so you could have access to Mexico and José. Well, forget that. I have my *own* network now."

"The missing gems, you took them, didn't you?"

Noah grinned again. "Ah, I see someone has started to pay attention. I told you that José wasn't able to deliver as much so that I could keep some back for startup money. Worked like a charm—until you came on this cruise to check up on me. I knew my gig was up."

"Wait a second," Margot said. "You're done? Just like that?"

He looked at her with boredom. "For this cruise line, but I've already got new people lined up on another while *I* retire. But don't worry, I've got a place for you." She hated the way he said it, but was glad to see he was still talking. Now she needed him to admit to what happened on board the ship. To the murders.

"What about me?" Brice asserted.

"I took care of everyone else, I'll take care of you."

Margot backed up, as if afraid. "What are you talking about?"

"Don't worry," Noah said, "I usually take very good care of my partners—as long as they aren't double-crossing me. I found out Kirsten was planted by a rival gang." Margot recognized the undercover story Gabe had told her they'd created. "And I couldn't leave any loose ends so Michael had to go too, thanks to a few gang members in Ensenada that respond well to cash. You see..." He looked back at Margot. "I take care of my own business. I don't force others to do it." Now he looked back at Brice, who looked appropriately shocked.

"But, what about our deal?" Brice stammered.

"Speaking of my own business, there *is* one more thing I need to take care of." He lifted the gun at Brice and pulled the trigger.

MARGOT SCREAMED, covering her head with her hands and cowering in front of Noah. She looked back at Brice, but he lay on the ground.

"Get down!" a voice screamed into her earpiece.

She obeyed and dropped to the floor just as a barrage of men in swat uniforms flooded the area. Shaking on the floor, Margot cowered on the other side of where Brice had fallen.

"Put the gun down!" a burly officer shouted at Noah. He looked around him, at the officers who all had guns trained on him, and finally moved to put the gun on the floor.

One officer moved forward and secured the weapon and

then two more came in and took hold of him as Adam raced into the small kitchen directly toward Margot.

"Are you all right?" he asked, looking down at her with his hands on both sides of her face.

She nodded. "B-Brice," she managed.

"I'm okay," came a voice from the other side of the island.

As Adam helped her to stand, she saw two officers helping him stand as well. One had pulled away his shirt to reveal the sturdy Kevlar vest that had caught the deadly bullet. She breathed a sigh of relief and nodded at him even as one officer put the handcuffs back on him. His negotiation to help them tonight would help him with his sentence, but he'd still need to do some jail time. She hoped that it would give him some time to think about what he'd done and to make his sister proud in his future decisions.

Adam wrapped his arm around Margot and pulled her toward the door just as Gabe came in.

"Great job, Margot," he said, nodding at her. He now wore a jacket with the initials DEA on the front. She narrowed her eyes at it and he shrugged. "So maybe I'm not FBI, but I used to be." He winked at Adam then took her hand in both of his. "Thank you again for what you were willing to do. You gave us the time we needed to gain the evidence to put Noah away."

"I'm glad. I also have a feeling you'll find all the other evidence you need in the flour sacks."

"What?" Gabe looked over his shoulder to where Margot was pointing.

"When I came on board here in Long Beach, Addie had it out with Michael Bowers about the fact that her flour hadn't been delivered. He said he took care of it, but then when we were in Ensenada, I came in to find more flour being loaded. I have a feeling it's either not flour or the drugs and gems are hidden in the flour."

"We'll check it out," he said with a nod. "Thanks for the tip. Now you guys go enjoy Long Beach. I hope it's restful and you can put this whole thing behind you."

Margot laughed. If only she and Adam could have a normal vacation experience, but she had a feeling that would never be the case.

They walked down the gangplank to the waiting Mustang convertible.

"You still have this?" she said, incredulous.

"Of course," he said with a grin. "I may have come down to Mexico for a few days but I wasn't about to give this beauty up just for that."

"By the way," she said, looking at him when they were seated, "how *did* you manage to get to Mexico, and on such short notice?"

Adam looked at her for a moment then turned his gaze back to the road. "It's a long story."

"Does it have something to do with how you know Gabe?"

"Um hum," was all he said.

She knew he was holding something back, the same thing he'd been holding back when she asked him what Gabe had meant at the restaurant. What was it about Adam's past that he didn't want her to know?

"Adam," she began, trying to find the right words, "I understand there are things you don't exactly want to share with me, but sometimes..." How could she put it? "Sometimes I feel like there is a whole part of you that I just don't know."

They drove in silence for a long time, the blare of an occasional horn the only disruption to the windswept quiet, but when they pulled up in front of her sister's house, he turned off the engine and turned toward her.

"Margie," he took her hand, holding it between both of his, "I care for you a lot. I hope you know that. I hope that you can *see* that. But..." He pressed his lips together in thought for a moment. "But there are some things I can't tell you. At least not yet. I hate that—I really do—but you have to trust me that I'll tell you when I can."

She nodded slowly. She understood, and yet she didn't. What was so important that he couldn't tell her about it? Was he working undercover? Was it something to do with his job? His past? His present? What was so important that Adam Eastwood had to keep it secret? He hadn't said it was classified, so aside from that, she didn't know what else it could be that he couldn't share.

Letting out a sigh, she gently pulled her hand from him. "I'm just disappointed you feel like you can't share this with me, that I'm not trustworthy enough. Good night, Adam."

He watched her go, his hazel eyes following her all the way up to the front of the house. When she turned around, she saw that he hadn't moved, his eyes still on hers. Then she stepped inside the house, closing the door on him.

# CHAPTER 13

THEY ALL SAT at a large table on the patio of the *La Playa* restaurant. Margot, Adam, her sister Renee, her husband Dillon, and Taylor. Even Addie and Grayson had come for the farewell brunch. After a week of shopping, visiting Disneyland, going to the beach and trying to surf with Taylor and her friends, Margot was ready to head back to the East Coast.

She missed her shop and, though she was kept in the loop from Dexter and assured that everything was going well, she wanted to be back to her regular schedule. Vacations were good, but they weren't real.

She thought back on the debriefing meetings she'd had with Gabe and Adam as well. Noah was being charged with two counts of murder along with his drug and gem smuggling, and she felt better knowing that his contacts on the other ships had been found and removed. Brice had also been sentenced to five years in prison with hopes of getting out earlier on bail for good behavior. She hoped he would turn his life around.

The notion that the gem and drug smuggling had ended, along with cooperation with the Mexican officials in Ensenada, filled Margot with contentment, but the fact that lives had been lost saddened her. There was no end to crime and destruction in this world, but she was glad she could have played a small part in ending some of it—even while on vacation.

Renee had just told a joke but Margot didn't laugh. She hadn't heard it and she could tell that Adam knew she was lost in another world.

"Hey," he said, leaning close, "let's take a walk."

Margot was torn. Looking around the circle of friends and family, she didn't want to leave them alone, but she desperately wanted to clear up the stuffiness that had descended between her and Adam.

At the same moment, Addie looked her way. "I'm sorry," she said, leaning forward, "but Grayson and I need to head out. We're meeting his mom tonight in Oxnard and we want to leave ourselves enough time to get out of the city."

"Of course! It was so good to see you." Margot embraced her friend as Adam shook Grayson's hand.

"He's a good guy," Addie whispered into her ear, "whatever it is that's going on, talk to him about it."

She leaned back and looked at her friend. "How—?"

"It takes one to know one," Addie said with a laugh. "All relationships are rocky, but I think you guys are suited for one another. I hope things work out."

Margot found herself hoping they would as well. She said good-bye to Grayson and then told Renee that they would meet her back at her house later. Then, slipping off their shoes, she and Adam set off on the beach.

They walked for a short time before he spoke up. "I was worried sick when I got that email from you."

"How did you know something was going on?" In the back of her mind, she was suspicious. She hadn't said anything particular to tip him off—or at least she hadn't *thought* she had—but now she was wondering if he'd known more about the situation. If he'd known Gabe—

She stopped herself. She *knew* Adam. Knew he was a good guy. Knew that he wouldn't do anything to hurt her. And yet here she was questioning his every move. She huffed out a breath and turned to look at him as they walked along the water's edge.

"I just had a feeling. Honestly…" He gave a humorless laugh. "Any time you ask me questions about things, I get the sense you're trying to pry information from me without coming out and telling me the truth." He eyed her with a look and she dropped her gaze.

He was right. Here she was, demanding that he be honest

with her—which was a good thing—and yet she hadn't come out and told him the truth either.

Sighing, she reached over and took his hand in hers as they walked. "I'm sorry, Adam. At the time, I only had suspicions. I didn't know for sure that anything was going on."

"I know. And I didn't think too much about it until I found out what Gabe was doing."

"What?"

"I just had a feeling." He shook his head with a faint smile. "Gabe's always been a slippery one."

Margot laughed. "What does that mean?"

"He's a good guy, but he dips into a lot of different things and sometimes that's gotten him in trouble in the past. I should have known he was working on something undercover. It just fits."

Margot pressed her lips together, knowing what she needed to say, but fighting against saying it. She cared so much for Adam, but her own independence, something that had grown in the wake of Julian's death, was sometimes stronger than she knew what do to do with. When they reached a set of swings looking out toward the ocean, Adam led them over and they sat, swaying back and forth.

"Margot," he began, but she cut him off.

"I'm sorry, Adam." He looked surprised. "You've done nothing but help me and believe me in all situations. I…I know I ask too much of you sometimes. I know you don't mean to keep me in the dark about things. I suppose I just need to have more patience. If you say you'll tell me when you can, then I need to believe you. Will you accept my apology?"

He smiled back at her, reaching out and clasping her hand in between the swings. "Of course. Just know that I care—very deeply—about you. There are things I want to share, but…I just can't yet. I will when I can. I promise."

Despite the desire to demand answers and her tendency to grow frustrated, she took a deep breath and nodded back at him. The look on his face was genuine and filled with care—for her.

She turned her gaze back to the ocean as they swung in tandem, hands held between the seats. She felt like a school girl again, if only for a moment, and she relished the innocent nature of what life looked like from the simple viewpoint of sand, sea, and sky.

# THANK YOU!

Thanks for reading *Pastries and Pilfering*. I hope you enjoyed reading the story as much as I enjoyed writing it. If you did, it would be awesome if you left a review for me on Amazon and/or Goodreads.

If you would like to know about future cozy mysteries by me and the other authors at Fairfield Publishing, make sure to sign up for our Cozy Mystery Newsletter. We will send you our FREE Cozy Mystery Starter Library just for signing up. All the details are on the next page.

At the very end of the book, I have included a couple previews of books by friends and fellow authors at

Fairfield Publishing. First is a preview of *Up in Smoke* by Shannon VanBergen - it's the first book in the Glock Grannies Cozy Mystery series. Second is a preview of *A Pie to Die For* by Stacey Alabaster - it's part of the popular Bakery Detectives Cozy Mystery series. I really hope you like the samples. If you do, both books are available on Amazon.

- Get Up in Smoke here: **amazon.com/dp/B06XHKYRRX**

- Get A Pie to Die For here: **amazon.com/dp/B01D6ZVT78**

## FAIRFIELD COZY MYSTERY NEWSLETTER

Make sure you sign up for the Fairfield Cozy Mystery Newsletter so you can keep up with our latest releases. When you sign up, **we will send you our FREE Cozy Mystery Starter Library!**

**FairfieldPublishing.com/cozy-newsletter/**

After you sign up to get your Free Starter Library, turn the page and check out the free previews :)

# PREVIEW: UP IN SMOKE

I COULD FEEL my hair puffing up like cotton candy in the humidity as I stepped outside the Miami airport. I pushed a sticky strand from my face, and I wished for a minute that it were a cheerful pink instead of dirty blond, just to complete the illusion.

"Thank you so much for picking me up from the airport." I smiled at the sprightly old lady I was struggling to keep up with. "But why did you say my grandmother couldn't pick me up?"

"I didn't say." She turned and gave me a toothy grin—clearly none of them original—and winked. "I parked over here."

When we got to her car, she opened the trunk and threw in the sign she had been holding when she met me in baggage claim. The letters were done in gold glitter glue and she had drawn flowers with markers all around the edges. My name "Nikki Rae Parker" flashed when the sun reflected off of them, temporarily blinding me.

"I can tell you put a lot of work into that sign." I carefully put my luggage to the side of it, making sure not to touch her sign—partially because I didn't want to crush it and partially because it didn't look like the glue had dried yet.

"Well, your grandmother didn't give me much time to make it. I only had about ten minutes." She glanced at the sign proudly before closing the trunk. She looked me in the eyes. "Let's get on the road. We can chit chat in the car."

With that, she climbed in and clicked on her seat belt. As I got in, she was applying a thick coat of bright red lipstick while looking in the rearview mirror. "Gotta look sharp in case we get pulled over." She winked again, her heavily wrinkled eyelid looking like it thought about staying closed before it sprung back up again.

I thought about her words for a moment. She must get

pulled over a lot, I thought. Poor old lady. I could picture her going ten miles an hour while the rest of Miami flew by her.

"Better buckle up." She pinched her lips together before blotting them slightly on a tissue. She smiled at me and for a moment, I was jealous of her pouty lips, every line filled in by layers and layers of red.

I did as I was told and buckled my seat belt before I sunk down into her caramel leather seats. I was exhausted, both physically and mentally, from the trip. I closed my eyes and tried to forget my troubles, taking in a deep breath and letting it out slowly to give all my worry and fear ample time to escape my body. For the first time since I had made the decision to come here, I felt at peace. Unfortunately, it was short-lived.

The sound of squealing tires filled the air and my eyes flung open to see this old lady zigzagging through the parking garage. She took the turns without hitting the brakes, hugging each curve like a racecar driver. When we exited the garage and turned onto the street, she broke out in laughter. "That's my favorite part!"

I tugged my seat belt to make sure it was on tight. This was not going to be the relaxing drive I had thought it would be.

We hit the highway and I felt like I was in an arcade game. She wove in and out of traffic at a speed I was sure matched her old age.

"Ya know, the older I get the worse other people drive." She took one hand off the wheel and started to rummage through her purse, which sat between us.

"Um, can I help you with something?" My nerves were starting to get the best of me as her eyes were focused more on her purse than the road.

"Oh no, I've got it. I'm sure it's in here somewhere." She dug a little more, pulling out a package of AA batteries and then a ham sandwich.

Brake lights lit up in front of us and I screamed, bracing myself for impact. The old woman glanced up and pulled the car to the left in a quick jerk before returning to her purse. Horns blared from behind us.

"There it is!" She pulled out a package of wintergreen Life Savers. "Do you want one?"

"No, thank you." I could barely get the words out.

"I learned a long time ago that it was easier if I just drove and did my thing instead of worrying about what all the other drivers were doing. It's easier for them to get out of my way instead of me getting out of theirs. My reflexes aren't what they used to be." She popped a mint in her mouth and smiled. "I love wintergreen. I don't know why peppermint is more popular. Peppermint is so stuffy; wintergreen is fun."

She seemed to get in a groove with her driving and soon my grip was loosening on the sides of the seat, the blood slowly returning to my knuckles. Suddenly I realized I hadn't asked her name.

"I was so confused when you picked me up from the airport instead of my Grandma Dean that I never asked your name."

She didn't respond, just kept her eyes on the road with a steely look on her face. I was happy to see her finally being serious about driving, so I turned to look out the window. "It's beautiful here," I said after a few minutes of silence. I turned to look at her again and noticed that she was still focused straight ahead. I stared at her for a moment and realized she never blinked. Panic rose through my chest.

"Ma'am!" I shouted as I leaned forward to take the wheel. "Are you okay?"

She suddenly sprung to action, screaming and jerking the wheel to the left. Her screaming caused me to scream and I grabbed the wheel and pulled it to the right, trying to get us back in our lane. We continued to scream until the car stopped teetering and settled down to a nice hum on the road.

"Are you trying to kill us?" The woman's voice was hoarse and she seemed out of breath.

"I tried to talk to you and you didn't answer!" I practically shouted. "I thought you had a heart attack or something!"

"You almost gave me one!" She flashed me a dirty look.

"And you made me swallow my mint. You're lucky I didn't choke to death!"

"I'm sorry." As I said the words, I noticed my heart was beating in my ears. "I really thought something had happened to you."

She was quiet for a moment. "Well, to be honest with you, I did doze off for a moment." She looked at me, pride spreading across her face. "I sleep with my eyes open. Do you know anyone who can do that?"

Before I could answer, she was telling me about her friend Delores who "claimed" she could sleep with her eyes open but, as it turned out, just slept with one eye half-open because she had a stroke and it wouldn't close all the way.

I sat there in silence before saying a quick prayer. My hands resumed their spot around the seat cushion and I could feel the blood draining from my knuckles yet again.

"So what was it you tried to talk to me about before you nearly killed us?"

I swallowed hard, trying to push away the irritation that fought to come out.

"I asked you what your name was." I stared at her and decided right then that I wouldn't take my eyes off of her for the rest of the trip. I would make sure she stayed awake, even if it meant talking to her the entire time.

"Oh yes! My name is Hattie Sue Miller," she said with a bit of arrogance. She glanced at me. "My father used to own most of this land." She motioned to either side of us. "Until he sold it and made a fortune." She gave me a look and dropped her voice to a whisper as she raised one eyebrow. "Of course we don't talk about money. That would be inappropriate." She said that last part like I had just asked her when she had last had sex. I felt ashamed until I realized I had never asked her about her money; I had simply asked her name. This woman was a nut. Didn't Grandma Dean have any other friends she could've sent to get me?

For the next hour or so, I asked her all kinds of questions to keep her awake—none of them about money or anything I thought might lead to money. If what she told me was true, she had a very interesting upbringing. She claimed to be related to Julia Tuttle, the woman who founded Miami. Her stories of how she got a railroad company to agree to build tracks there were fascinating. It wasn't until she told me she was also related to Michael Jackson that I started to question how true her stories were.

"We're almost there! Geraldine will be so happy to see you. You're all she's talked about the last two weeks." She pulled into a street lined with palm trees. "You're going to love it here." She smiled as she drove. "I've lived here a long time. It's far enough away from the city that you don't have all that hullaballoo, but big enough that you can eat at a different restaurant every day for a month."

When we entered the downtown area, heavy gray smoke

hung in the air, and the road was blocked by a fire truck and two police cars.

"Oh no! I think there might have been a fire!" I leaned forward in my seat, trying to get a better look.

"Of course there was a fire!" Hattie huffed like I was an idiot. "That's why Geraldine sent me to get you!"

"What?! Is she okay?" I scanned the crowd and saw her immediately. She was easy to spot, even at our distance.

"Oh yes. She's fine. Her shop went up in flames as she was headed out the door. She got the call from a neighboring store owner and called me right away to go get you. Honestly, I barely had time to make you a sign." She acted like Grandma Dean had really put her in a bad position, leaving her only minutes to get my name on a piece of poster board.

Hattie pulled over and I jumped out; I'd come back for my luggage later. As I made my way toward the crowd, I was amazed at how little my Grandma Dean—or Grandma Dean-Dean, as I had called her since I was a little girl—had changed. Her bleach blonde hair was nearly white and cut in a cute bob that was level with her chin. She wore skintight light blue denim capris, which hugged her tiny frame. Her bright white t-shirt was the background for a long colorful necklace that appeared to be a string of beads. Thanks to a pair of bright red heels, she stood eye to eye with the fireman she was talking to.

I ran up to her and called out to her. "Grandma! Are you

okay?" She flashed me a look of disgust before she smiled weakly at the fireman and said something I couldn't make out.

She turned her back to him and grabbed me by the arm. "I told you to never call me that!" She softened her tone then looked me over. "You look exhausted! Was it the flight or riding with that crazy Hattie?" She didn't give me time to answer. "Joe, this is my daughter's daughter, Nikki."

Joe smiled. I wasn't sure if it was his perfectly white teeth that got my attention, his uniform or his sparkling blue eyes, but I was immediately speechless. I tried to say hello, but the words stuck in my throat.

"Nikki, this is Joe Dellucci. He was born in New Jersey but his parents came from Italy. Isn't that right, Joe?"

I was disappointed when Joe answered without a New Jersey accent. Grandma Dean continued to tell me about Joe's heritage, which reminded me of Hattie. Apparently once you got to a certain age, you automatically became interested in people's backgrounds.

He must have noticed the look of disappointment on my face. "My family moved here when I was ten. My accent only slips in when I'm tired." His face lit up with a smile, causing mine to do the same. "Or when I eat pizza." I had no idea what he meant by that, but it caused me to break out in nervous laughter. Grandma Dean's look of embarrassment finally snapped me out of it.

"Well, Miss Dean. If I hear anything else, I'll let you know.

In the meantime, call your insurance company. I'm sure they'll get you in touch with a good fire restoration service. If not, let me know. My brother's in the business."

He handed her a business card and I saw the name in red letters across the front: *Clean-up Guys*. Not a very catchy name. Then suddenly it hit me. A fireman with a brother who does fire restoration? Seemed a little fishy. Joe must have noticed my expression, because he chimed in. "Our house burned down when I was eight and Alex was twelve. I guess it had an impact on us."

Grandma Dean took the card and put it in her back pocket. "Thanks, Joe. I'll give Alex a call this afternoon."

They said their good-byes and as Joe walked away, Grandma Dean turned toward me. "What did I tell you about calling me 'Grandma' in public?" Her voice was barely over a whisper. "I've given you a list of names that are appropriate and I don't understand why you don't use one of them!"

"I'm not calling you Coco!" My mind tried to think of the other names on the list. Peaches? Was that on there? Whatever it was, they all sounded ridiculous.

"There is nothing wrong with Coco!" She pulled away from me and ran a hand through her hair as a woman approached us.

"Geraldine, I'm so sorry to hear about the fire!" The woman hugged Grandma Dean. "Do they know what started it?"

"No, but Joe's on it. He'll figure it out. I'm sure it was wiring or something. You know how these old buildings are."

The woman nodded in agreement. "If you need anything, please let me know." She hugged Grandma again and gave her a look of pity.

"Bev, this is my...daughter's daughter, Nikki."

I rolled my eyes. She couldn't even say granddaughter. I wondered if she would come up with some crazy name to replace that too.

"It's nice to meet you," Bev said without actually looking at me. She looked worried. Her drawn-on eyebrows were pinched together, creating a little bulge between them. "If you hear anything about what started it, please be sure to let me know."

Grandma turned to me as the woman walked away. "She owns the only other antique store on this block. I'm sure she's happy as a clam that her competition is out for a while," Grandma said, almost with a laugh.

I gasped. "Do you think she did it? Do you think she set fire to your shop?"

"Oh, honey, don't go jumping to conclusions like that. She would never hurt a fly." Grandma looked around. "Where's your luggage?"

I turned to point toward Hattie's car, but it was gone.

Grandma let out a loud laugh. "Hattie took off with your luggage? Well, then let's go get it."

THANKS FOR READING the sample of *Up in Smoke*. I really hope you liked it. You can read the rest at:

- **amazon.com/dp/B06XHKYRRX**

MAKE sure you turn to the next page for the preview of *A Pie to Die For*.

# PREVIEW: A PIE TO DIE FOR

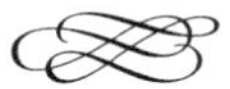

"BUT YOU DON'T UNDERSTAND, I use only the finest, organic ingredients." My voice was high-pitched as I pleaded my case to the policeman. Oh, this was just like an episode of Criminal Point. Hey, I wondered who the killer turned out to be. I shook my head. That's not important, Rachael, I scolded myself. *What's important is getting yourself off this murder charge.* Still, I hoped Pippa had recorded the ending of the episode.

I tried to steady my breathing as Jackson—Detective Whitaker—entered the room and threw a folder on the table, before studying the contents as though he was cramming for a test he had to take the next day. He rubbed his temples and frowned.

*Is he even going to make eye contact with me? Is he just going to completely ignore the interaction we had at the fair? Pretend it never even happened.*

"Jackson..." I started, before I was met with a steely glare. "Detective. Surely you can't think I had anything to do with this?"

Jackson looked up at me slowly. "Had you ever had any contact with Mrs. Batters before today?"

I shifted in my seat. "Yes," I had to admit. "I knew her a little from the store. She was always quite antagonistic towards me, but I'd never try to kill her!"

"Witnesses near the scene said that you two had an argument." He gave me that same steely glare. Where was the charming, flirty, sweet guy I'd meet earlier? He was now buried beneath a suit and a huge attitude.

"Well...it wasn't an argument...she was just...winding me up, like she always does."

Jackson shot me a sharp look. "So, she was annoying you? Was she making you angry?"

"Well... Well..." I tripped over my words. He was now making me nervous for an entirely different reason than he had earlier. Those butterflies were back, but now they felt like daggers.

*Come on, Rach. Everyone knows that the first suspect in Criminal Point is not the one that actually did it.*

But how many people had Jackson already interviewed? Maybe he was saving me for last. Gosh, maybe my cherry pie had actually killed the woman!

"Answer the question please, Miss Robinson."

"Not angry, no. I was just frustrated."

"Frustrated?" A smile curled at his lips before he pounced. "Frustrated with Mrs. Batters?"

"No! The situation. Come on—you were there!" I tried to appeal to his sympathies, but he remained a brick wall.

"It doesn't matter whether I was there or not. That is entirely besides the point." He said the words a little too forcefully.

I swallowed. "I couldn't get any customers to try my cakes, and Bakermatic was luring everyone away with their free samples." I stopped as my brows shot up involuntarily. "Jackson! Sorry, Detective. Mrs. Batters ate at Bakermatic as well!"

My words came out in a stream of breathless blabber as I raced to get them out. "Bakermatic must be to blame! They cut corners, they use cheap ingredients. Oh, and I know how much Mrs. Batters loved their food! She was always eating there. Believe me, she made that very clear to me."

Jackson sat back and folded his arms across his chest. "Don't try to solve this case for us."

I sealed my lips. *Looks like I might have to at this rate.*

"We are investigating every place Mrs. Batters ate today. You don't need to worry about that."

I leaned forward and banged my palm on the table. "But I do need to worry about it! This is my job, my livelihood… my life on the line. If people think I am to blame, that will be the final nail in my bakery's coffin!" Oh, what a day. And I'd thought it was bad enough that I hadn't gotten any customers at my stand. Now I was being accused of killing a woman!

I could have sworn I saw a flicker of sympathy finally crawl across Jackson's face. He stood up and readjusted his tie, but he still refused to make full eye contact. "You're free to go, Miss Robinson," he said gently. There was that tone from earlier, finally. He seemed recognizable as a human at long last.

"Really?"

He nodded. "For the moment. But we might have some more questions for you later, so don't leave town."

I tried to make eye contact with him as I left, squirreling out from underneath his arm as he held the door open for me, but he just kept staring at the floor.

Did that mean he wasn't coming back to my bakery after all?

~

PIPPA WAS STILL WAITING for me when I returned home later that evening. There was a chill in the air, which meant that I headed straight for a blanket and the fireplace when I finally crawled in through the door. Pippa shot me a sympathetic look as I curled up and crumbled in front of the flames. *How had today gone so wrong, so quickly?*

"I recorded the last part of the show," Pippa said softly. "If you're up for watching it."

I groaned and lay on the carpet, my back straight against the floor like I was a little kid. "I don't think I can stomach it after what I just went through. Can you believe it? Accusing ME of killing Mrs. Batters? When I *know* that Bakermatic is to blame. I mean, Pippa, they must be! But this detective wouldn't even listen to me when I was trying to explain Bakermatic's dodgy practices to him."

Pippa leaned forward and took the lid off a pot, the smell of the brew hitting my nose. "Pippa, what is that?"

She grinned and stirred it, which only made the smell worse. I leaned back and covered my nose. "Thought it might be a bit heavy for you. I basically took every herb, tea, and spice that you had in your cabinet and came up with this! I call it 'Pippa's Delight'!"

"Yeah well, it doesn't sound too delightful." I sat up and scrunched up my nose. "Oh, what the heck—pour me a cup."

"Are you sure?" Pippa asked with a cheeky grin.

"Go on. I'll be brave."

I braced myself as the brown liquid hit the white mug.

It was as disgusting as I had imagined, but at least it made me laugh when the pungent concoction hit my tongue. Pippa always had a way of cheering me up. If it wasn't her unusual concoctions, or her ever changing hair color—red this week but pink the last, and purple a week before that—then it was her never-ending array of careers and job changes that entertained me and kept me on my toes. When you're trying to run your own business, forced to be responsible day in and day out, you have to live vicariously through some of your more free-spirited friends. And Pippa was definitely that: free-spirited.

"Hey!" I said suddenly, as an idea began to brew in my brain. I didn't know if it was the tea that suddenly brought all my senses to life or what it was, but I found myself slamming my mug on the table with new found enthusiasm. "Pippa, have you got a job at the moment?" I could never keep up with Pippa's present state of employment.

She shrugged as she kicked her feet up and lay back on the sofa. "Not really! I mean, I've got a couple of things in the works. Why's that?"

I pondered for a moment. "Pippa, if you could get a job at Bakermatic, you could see first hand what they're up to!" My voice was a rush of excitement as I clapped my hands together. "You would get to find out the ways they cut corners, the bad ingredients they use, and, if you were really lucky, you might even overhear someone say something about Mrs. Batters!"

A gleam appeared in Pippa's green eyes. "Well, I do need a job, especially after today."

I raced on. "Yes! And you've got plenty of experience working in cafes."

"Yeah. I've worked in hundreds of places." She took a sip of the tea and managed to swallow it. She actually seemed to enjoy it.

"I know you've got a lot of experience. You're sure to get the job. They're always looking for part-timers." Unfortunately, Bakermatic was planning on expanding the storefront even further, and that meant they were looking for even more employees to fill their big yellow store. "Pippa, this is the perfect plan! We'll get you an application first thing in the morning. Then you can start investigating!"

Pippa raised her eyebrows. "Investigating?"

I nodded and lay my head back down on the carpet. "Criminal Point—Belldale Style! Bakery Investigation Unit! I will investigate and do what I can from my end as well! Perhaps I could talk to people from all the other food stalls! Oh, Pippa, we're going to make a crack team of detectives!"

"The Bakery Detectives!"

We both started giggling but, as the full weight of the day's events started to pile up on me, I felt my stomach tighten. It might seem fun to send Pippa in to spy on

Bakermatic, but this was serious. My bakery, my livelihood, and even my own freedom depended on it.

THANKS FOR READING a sample of my book, *A Pie to Die For*. I really hope you liked it. You can read the rest at:

**amazon.com/dp/B01D6ZVT78**

OR YOU CAN GET it for free by signing up for our newsletter.

**FairfieldPublishing.com/cozy-newsletter/**

**amazon.com/dp/B01D6ZVT78**

Made in the USA
Middletown, DE
08 November 2022